FOAL

SHE SHALL DIE

Even Hatty Savage had to admit at the inquest that it had been foolish of her, when Richard Sheridan had threatened suicide, to hand him her sleeping tablets. And when a girl who had apparently been trying to blackmail her also came to an abrupt end, Hatty found herself in custody.

Once the scandal and anonymous letters after the inquest died down, she had married Philip Cobb, a local solicitor. When Hatty was locked up, Philip enlists the help of the famous investigator Arthur Crook — a good idea he thought, until the investigator seemed to be regarding him as the prime suspect.

SHE SHALL DIE

Anthony Gilbert

·BLACK·
DAGGER
·CRIME·

First published 1961
by
William Collins, Sons & Co. Ltd.

This edition 2003 by Chivers Press
published by arrangement with
the author's estate

ISBN 0 7540 8643 7

British Library Cataloguing in Publication Data available

Printed and bound in Great Britain by
Antony Rowe Ltd., Chippenham, Wiltshire

CHAPTER I

ON THE DAY that Richard Sheridan died Henrietta Savage heard her daughter come home in the small hours. She switched on a bedside lamp and saw that it was two-thirty ; she left the light on in case Hatty wanted to look in, but the steps went quickly along the passage and a minute later a closed door warned her that Hatty had gone to bed. She sighed a little.

" Hatty having one of her moods," she thought. They had been particularly frequent of late. Another man, she supposed. Hatty did everything with such energy. At least it meant she had got over Richard, and that would please her father. John Savage had come up the hard way, " and I didn't work sixteen hours a day for a young blade like that to hang up his hat on a golden hook behind my door."

As though John wouldn't do anything for Hatty, she thought, smiling. All the same, she couldn't help feeling that all this chopping and changing was going to make just one man, a husband, say, seem pretty monotonous.

It was ten o'clock before Hatty came down next day, and then she was dressed for the street, smart topcoat and a great white fur hat like a beehive. An absurd fashion thought Henrietta, but she had to admit the style hadn't been invented that could make her look ridiculous or plain.

" Oh, Hatty, you can't go out without breakfast," she protested.

" Just some coffee," said Hatty. She poured herself a cup from the pot on the hotplate.

" That'll be half cold."

" Oh, Mother, don't fuss. It's all right."

Henrietta slipped a couple of slices of bread into the electric toaster.

" Where are you going ? "

" It's my clinic morning. If I'm late Mrs. Addison won't

5

say anything, but I shall know what she's thinking. These volunteers! No sense of responsibility."

"Oh, nonsense," said Henrietta. "She thinks very well of you."

"Too kind," murmured Hatty, and the toast popped up, a pale golden brown.

"Nice party last night?" asked Henrietta, picking up her pencil. She didn't expect any answer. Hatty always said, "It was all right. Why, did you expect something to happen?" The answer came with such regularity that Henrietta had stopped listening for it. So it was a shock— to be the first of many, though she didn't realise it then— when Hatty said nothing. Henrietta looked up; something was wrong, but she had too much sense to ask what it was. Instead she inquired lightly, "Is there anyone you want specially asked for the next Cold Comfort party?"

Hatty's face changed; her head tipped back, even her voice had a kind of new bloom on it.

"Oh, Mother, would you send a card to Alan Duke? I don't know his address, but he's a friend of the Ainslies. They'd forward it."

"Alan Duke." Dutifully Henrietta inscribed the name. "Have I met him?"

"I shouldn't think so. This will be your chance."

Henrietta nodded; she had long ago ceased to try and keep count of all her daughter's friends; sometimes she wondered if Hatty could put a name to them all.

"Oh, and by the way," said Hatty, "you needn't ask Richard this time."

Henrietta dropped her pencil again. "Not ask Richard Sheridan? Of course I shall. Alison would be terribly hurt if we left him out."

Hatty crashed down her cup so that the saucer cracked. "So, because Alison's going to be hurt, you've got to go on inviting people here even if they bore me to death."

"I can remember a time when you were anything but bored by Richard," Henrietta observed, unwisely. "Everyone thought . . ."

"I'm not responsible for what people think. It's a pity

they haven't got something better to do. Anyway, if you ask Richard here I shan't be at the party, and you needn't ask Alan either."

Henrietta thought for a moment. " Hatty, was Richard there last night ? "

" Richard's always there."

" And—you had a row ? "

" If you must know," cried Hatty desperately, " he proposed."

Henrietta could scarcely repress a laugh. " Well, that's not an insult. You don't have to accept it."

" I shouldn't dream of accepting him. I wouldn't marry Richard for all the tea in China. Just because you think the world of Alison Sheridan, that doesn't mean her nephew's the Archangel Michael."

Henrietta perceived something pretty serious had occurred.

" Hatty, you must give me some better reason . . ."

" What better reason is there ? When I said Don't be silly —oh, Mother, he nearly had hysterics. I thought he was going to upset the car. One thing, I'll never give him a lift again."

" All right," said Henrietta, " since you make such a point of it. But that doesn't mean I'm going to drop the Sheridans. I've an immense admiration for Alison, and don't forget, Richard works in your father's bank."

" Well, he won't much longer. He told me that. He's got everything laid on, he's going to be a tycoon."

" You mean, he's going in with Alison at The Clover House, after all ? I always thought he was silly not to. That restaurant's a little gold-mine."

" I shouldn't think so," said Hatty. " Alison believes in starting from the bottom of the ladder. Can you see Richard washing dishes ? "

" It's how Alison started. You're all so impatient nowadays."

" What else can you expect, with the shadow of the atombomb hanging over us ? There isn't any time . . . Oh, and talking of time, look at the clock."

She grabbed her gloves and ran for the door. " Richard will be all right. He's only twenty-one, silly to think of getting married anyway. Though I know he thinks it was rather unfair of his father to leave everything to Alison."

" She's stood *in loco parentis* to him most of his life, even before his parents were killed in an air-raid. And she's put the money to excellent account. Richard will inherit everything in due course."

" He doesn't want it in due course, he wants it now, and I can't say I blame him. Alison's the kind that will live to be ninety. Anyway, she might be grateful to me, leaving her ewe lamb in the fold a little longer. Married men don't have much time for their aunts."

" Don't be surprised if people talk," Henrietta warned her.

" I hate living in a village, there's no privacy. Oh, well, perhaps I'll give them something to talk about soon."

" Hatty, you're not trying to tell me you're engaged or anything like that ? "

" I'm not telling you anything. Oh, sometimes I wish I had a flat or something and could walk as far as the pillar-box without everybody speculating who I was writing to."

She went out, slamming the door behind her, and Henrietta heard her starting up her little white car.

" In love and not sure of her man," decided Henrietta. " Nothing's more infuriating than getting a proposal from the wrong man when you're longing for one from someone else."

She wondered about this Alan Duke ; it was Victorian to expect references these days, but sometimes she thought the Victorians had quite a lot of sense on their side.

Mrs. Addison had been at it for twenty minutes when Hatty's little cream-coloured roadster drew up outside the clinic. Hatty left her coat and gloves in the car but she kept on the white fur beehive. As usual, the place was approaching pandemonium. Only mothers with children in arms were supposed to attend, but you couldn't leave the two and three and four-year-olds at home, and everyone hadn't got a Mum or a kindly neighbour, and there wasn't an infant school here for the over-threes, and no crèches, of course. So the corridor leading to the clinic was littered with push-carts and children's coats and toys. Model railway engines and cars were being scraped with hideous dissonance up and down the passage, tots, male and female alike, let off Davy Crockett guns, patted coloured balloons from hand to hand or wound up clockwork dogs and monkeys. In one corner a nice girl of seventeen was manipulating a puppet in the fruitless hope of preserving some semblance of quiet, but it was a mistake really, because the children crowded round her trying to snatch it out of her hands and screaming when she withdrew it from reach.

" Don't care about her silly old puppet," yelled one boy, scornfully. " They do it a lot better on the telly."

As Hatty threaded her way up the crowded corridor she heard one or two sniggers from the Mums who thought her hat a perfect scream. They all knew she came voluntarily, and many of them assumed that for this reason she thought herself a cut above them.

" Not that anyone 'ud *pay* her just to hold a baby," they confided, " and if it wasn't for us she wouldn't know what to do with herself."

Hatty did clerical work here, noting names and addresses, and making records ; when she got back she'd type them out and later she and one or two other volunteers might do a bit of visiting. Not that she was very successful at this. The mums didn't have much faith in an unmarried woman, whatever her age. It stood to reason if you hadn't had a husband you'd no notion what life could do to you.

It was an unexpectedly busy morning. Mums who'd hitherto scorned what they called the amatoors suddenly appeared, they brought children who had nothing conceivable wrong with them, the gossip in the corridor swelled like a crowd of bees.

" Has a rumour gone round that we're having a distribution of free gifts ? " Mrs. Addison murmured. " Why are they all here ? "

The new-comers seemed to regard Hatty with particular interest, but nothing really blew up, as it were, until a Mrs.

Chadwick, seeing Hatty about to pick up her child, which was beautiful enough to have come out of a fairy-tale, snatched it back.

" I wasn't going to pinch her," said Hatty, using the word in its original meaning.

" I'm able to manage my own child, thank you," snapped Mrs. Chadwick.

Presently Hatty left the clinic and went towards a door marked Toilet, and all the heads in the passage turned to watch her. Another mum came in while she was away who, handing over her child, a rampageous red-head, leaned across to whisper something to Mrs. Addison.

" Who says so ? " inquired Mrs. Addison sharply.

" It's all over the place," said the mum. " Hadn't you heard ? "

" I was here at nine o'clock," Mrs. Addison pointed out. " We're changing the filing system and that means a lot of clerical work, you know."

" I can't see how a filing system helps baby," said the mum with brisk finality.

" You'd think she'd have the decency to stop away, wouldn't you ? " she added.

" I don't know what you're talking about," Mrs. Addison assured her. " That'll do. Take Ava away." (Ava indeed! Once it had been Marlene, and several of the mums were called Greta.)

Then Hatty came back, walking as gracefully as a young deer. " That girl may spend a fortune on her clothes," Mrs. Addison reflected, " but it pays her handsome interest." She was an arresting type, tall and slender, with a fineness of bone structure that would outlast all the ravages of age. She had her mother's dark hair, but her eyes were a deep blue that looked black when emotion swayed her ; good hands, she might have made a doctor, Mrs. Addison thought. No, she decided, she hasn't heard, and yet something's wrong. Another mum was coming in, so she couldn't ask the burning question, and before she found an opportunity there was an interruption so unexpected that even the mums' tongues were silenced for an instant. Tedder, an ex-A.R.P.

warden, who stood duty on the door on these occasions, came in and hesitated.

" What is it, Mr. Tedder ? " Mrs. Addison asked.

" Miss Savage is wanted on the telephone."

" Can't you take a message ? " inquired Hatty. " No one's supposed to ring me up here."

Tedder looked doubtful but he moved away. A minute later he was back.

" It's Mr. Savage. He says will you come home at once ? "

" My father ? Did he say why ? "

" Just that it was urgent."

" You go at once, Hatty," said Mrs. Addison. " Pamela can take over here."

She called the girl who had been playing with the puppet.

" It's Mother," decided Henrietta, picking up her bag. " Something's happened to Mother." Suddenly she felt as cold as the Ice Maiden.

Running the gauntlet of the assembled intensely curious, shamelessly excited mums was like walking the plank, she thought. She said in a sudden loud voice, " My mother's ill," and there was a momentary silence, almost a flush of shame. But as the door swung behind her, one mum said to the next, " Of course, they have to say that, but the Savages are silly if they think they can hush this up."

When she reached the house the front door opened and her father appeared. She ran up the drive saying, " Is it Mother ? What's happened ? " Then for the first time she saw there was someone standing behind him, a square-shouldered man in a dark suit, whom she did not know.

" Nothing's happened to your mother," said John Savage. " That is, she's shocked, of course, as everyone's bound to be, as you're going to be. This is Inspector Ferrers."

Hatty stared, shaking her head in its fantastic beehive hat.

" What have the police got to do with it, whatever it is ? "

" We'd better come into my study," said Savage. " I take it, Inspector, there'll be no objection to my remaining in the room while you ask my daughter whatever questions you have in mind ? "

" It's irregular," said Ferrers.

" Then I must ask you to wait while I telephone our lawyer."

Hatty spun round. " What is all the mystery ? For goodness' sake, someone tell me."

The two men exchanged glances. Then Ferrers said, " I believe Mr. Richard Sheridan is a friend of yours, Miss Savage ? "

" Well, I know him, of course. Everyone does. What's happened ? "

The inspector said, " He was found dead in his bed this morning, and as you were the last person so far as we can ascertain to see him alive . . ."

He didn't finish his sentence. The girl's face had assumed so chalky a pallor that even the policeman was shocked. He had seen dead bodies often enough, both in the war and out of it, but here was something to appal the heart. It was as if all the blood had receded from the brain taking every vestige of energy from the vigorous flesh. John caught his daughter's arm.

" Sit down. I'll get you a drop of brandy." He opened a cupboard and found a glass. " There's nothing for you to be afraid of," he said urgently. " This is simply routine, as the inspector will assure you. He's going to ask you . . ."

" I'll take over if you don't mind, Mr. Savage. Miss Savage, when did you last see Mr. Sheridan ? "

" About two o'clock this morning, I suppose." She took the glass from her father's hand and sipped the contents ; a little warmth flowed through her frozen veins. " I dropped him at the corner of Allen Lane. That's only a step from where he lives. He doesn't have his own car," she added explanatorily to the inspector. " One of us generally gives him a lift if we're out in the evening."

" Did he seem his usual self then ? "

Hatty hesitated. Then she said with a shrug, " I expect Mother's told you this already. He asked me to marry him last night and when I said I wouldn't he got very excited."

" How excited, Miss Savage ? I mean, can you remember anything he said ? "

" Oh, he went on and on, about my giving him encourage-
ment and not being able to live if I didn't accept him,
and . . ."

" You're sure he said that, about not being able to live ? "

" Yes."

" Did you take that seriously ? "

" Of course I didn't."

" Did you ever hear him say he had sleeping-tablets ? "
the inspector asked.

She lifted her ghastly face towards him. " Is *that* what it
was ? "

" The post-mortem is being performed this afternoon,
but Dr. Wales has no doubt that he died of an overdose of
one of the barbiturates."

" Oh no," said Hatty. " He wouldn't do that. I mean,
it must have been an accident."

Ferrers watched her like a hawk.

" Miss Sheridan tells us that so far as she is aware he
never had any sleeping-tablets and she has never had them.
We've seen Dr. Wales, who was their physician, and he has
never prescribed any for either of them."

" Would he have to get them on a prescription ? I mean,
there are ways——"

" Such as ? "

Hatty put her head in her hands. " You must let me
think."

" I only want you to answer my questions, Miss Savage.
Have you any idea where he could have procured the
tablets ? "

She hesitated so long that he was about to put the question
again. Then she said, " Yes. He got them from me."

John Savage gave a violent start. " Think what you're
saying, my dear."

" How could I guess he was in earnest ? " she demanded.
" Oh, he became such a bore, all this talk about not being
able to carry on, and never trusting a woman again and
saying how sorry I'd be when he was dead, that I said,
' Oh, well, if you've made up your mind, I'll help you.'
And I had some sleeping-tablets and I gave them to him."

Savage said sharply, " I think at this stage I should call Mr. Arbuthnot. I believe my daughter has the right to refuse to answer questions without a lawyer being present."

" Mr. Arbuthnot couldn't make any difference to the facts," insisted Hatty. " That's what happened. I said, ' One is safe, two are dangerous and three are fatal.' "

" How many did you give him, Miss Savage ? "

" I gave him three. I only had four and I wanted one for myself. Well, so would anyone after that kind of scene. He really was quite something. If you saw that kind of thing on the stage——"

" What precisely was in the tablets ? " Ferrers bored away like a burying beetle.

" I don't know. I didn't get them from a doctor, someone gave me some. I know you're supposed to get them on prescriptions, but apparently if you're in the know it's not difficult."

" Who supplied them ? " The inspector might have been made of stone.

" I don't know. Oh, that's quite true. Some girl who had come down from London—Phoebe, Fenella, I can't even be sure of that and I never heard her surname—I happened to say, ' I know I shall never sleep to-night,' and she said, ' Well, take these, honey.' "

" How long ago was this ? "

" Oh, ages ago, months. I never saw her again. I don't even know who she came with. You know what these parties are."

The expression on the inspector's face said he didn't—thank God.

" Anyway, they were the only ones I had, and there weren't a great many."

" But you were accustomed to carrying them about with you ? "

" They looked rather like Veganin, and you know what these cleaning women are. They have a headache and they look round for aspirin or something, I didn't want to run any risks. They've been knocking about in my bag for a long time."

" And when a young man, whose offer of marriage has just been rejected and who is in an excitable state of mind, speaks of suicide you put the means into his hand ? Is that what you ask us to believe ? "

" Don't they say people who threaten to make a hole in the water are the ones who never do ? "

" It's not a very safe conclusion to draw. In this case . . ."

" He wouldn't do that because I refused him. I don't believe he was even in love with me."

Savage interposed, " My daughter seems to make sense to me, Inspector. After all, so long as she remained unengaged he could ask her again."

" Perhaps Miss Savage made it perfectly clear that in no circumstances . . ."

" If every man who couldn't marry the first woman he asked committed suicide," Hatty began.

The inspector intervened. " You had spent the evening with Mr. Sheridan, I understand ? "

" Well, it was a party and he was one of the members."

" How many were you ? "

" About ten."

" Can you give me the names of the others ? "

" Does it matter ? "

" It's important to establish his frame of mind."

Hatty gave him some names.

" You were all together all the evening ? "

" Well, most of the evening. We all began at the Magpie and then we went on to the Flower Garden—do you know it?—it's a perfectly respectable kind of road-house, with a cabaret, and we had dinner there and danced and then Richard and I went on to the King of Hearts on the Lewton Road for a final drink."

" Should you say, Miss Savage, you'd had a fair amount to drink ? "

" No more than average. I never drink very much, when I'm driving. Anyway, I don't like it particularly."

" And Mr. Sheridan ? "

" About the same as usual. It didn't matter so much for

him. He wasn't going to drive. And he always drank more than I did. But he was sober, if that's what you mean."

" Would you say his manner was any different from usual ? "

" He'd been tensed-up all evening."

" Perhaps because he was keying himself up to propose."

" You make it sound quite an ordeal."

" Would it surprise you to know that he hadn't mentioned this impending proposal to Miss Sheridan ? "

Hatty stared insolently. " Why should he ? He was of age. It was time enough to tell her when we were engaged. Anyway, she'd probably have told him not to make a fool of himself."

" You're suggesting that only a fool would have proposed ? "

" Only a fool would have made that sort of proposal. Why, he didn't even suggest we should be engaged. I said my father wouldn't agree, and he said, ' Well, why ask him ? Let's elope and present them with a *fait accompli.* ' I thought he'd gone mad. Why, he couldn't really keep himself . . ."

John's head came up with a jerk. " Hatty, do remember you'll have to repeat this in court. Are you sure that's what he said ? "

" Of course I'm sure."

" And how did he take your rejection of his offer, Miss Savage ? I mean, did he seem . . . ? "

" Suicidal ? I wouldn't have said so. He put on this act——"

" Did he speak of future plans, say, ' I'll ask you again later,' or . . . ? "

" I wasn't interested in his future plans. I've told you what he said."

" I see." The inspector doodled. " Miss Savage, there's something else I must ask you. Did he make any threats . . . ? "

" Threats ? What kind of threats could he make ? "

" I don't know, of course. But a man doesn't take an overdose . . ."

" It was an accident, I'm sure of it. He simply didn't

realise or didn't believe that three tablets would be fatal."

" Even though he'd been warned ? "

" He didn't have to believe me. I suppose he might have done it out of spite, but I don't believe that."

" It certainly doesn't sound like Richard," John agreed. Hatty veered abruptly.

" He didn't sound like himself last night."

Ferrer was as ruthless as the incoming tide.

"——didn't speak of having anything on his mind— besides this proposal you weren't disposed to accept ? We've seen Miss Sheridan, she says that so far as she knows he was under no financial stress."

Hatty shrugged. " I dare say she wouldn't have known if he had been."

"It's true that young men do commit suicide for romantic reasons . . ."

" Well, I call it very weak-kneed as well as very selfish. He could have put up a bit of a fight, tried a bit of a kidnapping or something a bit spirited. I hate people who just fold up."

The inspector doodled faster than ever. " Did he speak to you of any financial crisis ? "

" I didn't know there was one."

Ferrers hung on like a ferret pinning down an elusive rabbit.

" He didn't try and borrow money, anything like that ? "

" Borrow money from me ? Of course not. Alison Sheridan would never forgive him if he did. Anyway, I'm only a rich man's daughter, I'm not a rich woman in my own right. Besides, I didn't get the impression that money was worrying him. When I said what should we live on, he said he had something lined up, he didn't mean to be a bank clerk much longer."

" He didn't give you any idea . . . ? "

" I didn't listen, not very seriously. All I wanted to do was get back. Then we had all this stuff about putting an end to himself and I gave him the tablets."

" Yes. I don't want to harry you, Miss Savage, but could you be a little more explicit ? "

" How more explicit can anyone be ? He said ' You don't think I'd do it, do you ? ' and I said, 'Well, here's your chance,' or something like that."

" It must be obvious that my daughter is considerably upset by this news which has been broken to her very abruptly," said John Savage in a hard voice.

The inspector looked impenitent. " Sudden death is apt to be abrupt," he said. " Miss Savage, when you offered Mr. Sheridan the tablets, what did he say ? "

" He said, ' You think of everything, darling, don't you ? ' "

" There was no hesitation on his part in taking them ? "

" He took them all right. I thought for a minute he was going to throw them out of the window, but he didn't. He put them in his pocket. ' The only thing you ever gave me,' he said. ' I must keep that.' "

" And then ? "

" I said, ' Can you find your own way home if I put you down at the corner ? I'd as soon have a tiger in the car.' My nerves were a bit frayed, too," she added defiantly.

" Now—there's one more point, Miss Savage. You're quite certain he put the phial in his pocket ? "

" Yes. But I don't think he meant to kill himself. Why on earth should he ? If he'd really been in love he'd have thought of my feelings."

Ferrers stood up. " Thank you, Miss Savage. I needn't bother you any further. You realise, of course, you'll have to attend the inquest. Your father will advise you about being represented. By the way," he picked up his soft black hat, " you didn't say anything about this to anyone ? "

" I haven't seen anyone except my mother, unless you count Mrs. Addison. I just told her he'd proposed and there'd been a bit of a scene."

" You didn't speak of the tablets ? "

" She didn't even know I had them."

" Can I show you out, Inspector ? " John suggested.

" There's one point I'd like you to consider, Miss Savage," Ferrers said. (Does he have to say her name every time he opens his mouth ? thought John, irritably.) " You say you handed him the phial and then took it back because you wanted to retain one tablet for your own use ? "

" Yes. I'm afraid I can't show you that because I took it, and as I've just explained it was the last I had."

" You're quite sure you didn't give him the three tablets and retain the phial yourself ? "

" Quite sure. Why do you ask ? "

" Because we searched the house as soon as we realised what had happened and before there was an opportunity for anything to be disposed of, and there's no trace of a phial anywhere."

CHAPTER II

THE INQUEST on Richard Sheridan that was held in the Travellers' Inn at Brightling was packed. Even those present who hadn't known the young man were shocked by the news, and everyone knew Alison's successful venture. Then, too, rumour flies faster than a jet plane, and already Hatty's connection with the event was common knowledge. The girl came with her parents, wearing the same white beehive hat she had had on when she was summoned home.

" Cool as a cucumber," they said. A girl as pretty and as rich as she was is bound to have enemies, people who don't mind, from sheer spite, seeing her in trouble ; and Richard had been popular, had a gay, reckless way with him. Any number of young women would have closed with the offer to become Mrs. Richard Sheridan ; some of Hatty's own set thought the pair of them had been a cinch some months before, in the days when Alan Duke wasn't even a name. And a life lost—well, thrown away—for love still has a romantic ring.

When the court opened, practically no one had any thought of murder.

John Savage had arranged for his daughter to be represented by Philip Cobb, a partner of old Silas Arbuthnot, the family lawyer. " He'll do it better than I should," Arbuthnot declared. " He's an ambitious fellow and very reliable. Tell Hatty to follow his advice and she'll be all right, as right as she can hope for."

Hatty had met Philip Cobb a few times; Henrietta sometimes sent him a card for one of her larger parties. He was a shortish, sturdily-built man, with a pale, square face, dark hair and eyes, a mouth like a bull-terrier's. You'd never get anything away from him that he didn't choose to let go. Not handsome, said Henrietta, but unforgettable. Formidable, though, a thruster, a die-in-the-ditch fellow, and it was beginning to look as though that was just what Hatty was needing. Because the inquest turned out to be more terrible than she had dreamed.

Philip Cobb had primed her in advance. " Just answer questions," he said. " Don't volunteer any statements and don't add any embroidery. If anyone says, ' That's not what you told the inspector,' don't begin to argue. It's not reasonable for you to repeat your story word for word. And above all, don't forget you're in a tight spot. Young men killing themselves for love may be very romantic on the screen or in fiction, but it's not really well thought of in actuality."

He himself was calm enough.

" I can't change my story now," Hatty said rather sullenly. It seemed impossible that this appalling thing was happening to John Savage's lucky, beautiful girl. " I suppose if I'd had time to think I might have kept my mouth shut about the sleeping-pills, no one need ever have known . . ."

" I wouldn't be too sure of that." Philip Cobb sounded impassive. " He might have told his aunt."

" But she never saw him. She was in bed when he came back."

" You didn't know that at the time, though."

" No." Hatty considered. " Though he always said he told her not to sit up."

" He could have wakened her, though. No, you couldn't afford to take that chance. Only don't expect much sympathy from the jury. They're the usual hard-working crowd and they won't take a very friendly view of the situation. Rich girl leads poor young man on—no, I'm only telling you what they'll say, you may as well be prepared—and then ditches him when someone more attractive turns up."

" Why do you say that ? " Her breath came quickly and hard and the colour flew in her cheeks like a flag.

" You must remember you're not living in a big town where you can maintain a decent degree of privacy. Nothing in a village is private. You were going around everywhere with young Sheridan for a while, naturally tongues began to wag. It's one of the things tongues are for. Then you weren't going around with him in the same way. People notice. Now, if any questions are put to you that I consider impermissible I shall intervene on your behalf, but coroners are pretty well educated these days, and it won't do you any good to get on the wrong side of him. The sympathy of the court is going to be with Miss Sheridan— you probably feel sympathetic for her yourself—O.K., don't make any secret of it. Our case must be that the young man was spoilt and when he couldn't get what he wanted he started to make trouble. Your case, of course, is that it never went through your mind he'd take the pills. It was a gesture, an unfortunate one as it turned out, but he was of age, and he'd been warned. Whatever you do, don't antagonise the coroner. Things are sticky enough as it is."

Then he wished her luck.

Not even John Savage could realise how much she was going to need it.

It was Mrs. Groves, the Sheridans' daily, who had found the body. She told her story with a mixture of excitement and dismay that enthralled the court. On Wednesdays, she said, Miss Sheridan stopped in bed late. Being early closing at Brightling there was less trade being done than usual and, seeing the restaurant was open of a Sunday, Miss Sheridan took her rest-time on that morning. It was usual for Mrs. Groves to take her up a tray of orange juice and coffee and toast as soon as she arrived. This done, she took any orders there might be and went right along to Mr. Richard's room.

Other mornings, she explained, Miss Sheridan saw to breakfast for the pair of them.   Wednesdays Richard generally
got something to eat at a café near the station.

While the kettle boiled for tea she tidied up the kitchen.
Now and again the young man brought a friend back and
they had beer and a snack, after which the kitchen looked
as though a tornado had passed through it.   On this
particular morning, however, there was nothing to be
cleared away but a beer glass and an empty bottle.   She
washed the glass and put the bottle to go back with the
empties, then she made the coffee and carried the tray upstairs.   When she went into Richard Sheridan's room she
was surprised to find the curtains still drawn and the young
man still in bed.   She went to wake him up, to warn him he'd
overslept, but . . . " I saw at once how it was," she told the
jury, " and I went back to Miss Sheridan and asked her to
come along. ' He doesn't look right to me,' I said."   No,
there hadn't been a glass or any sign of a phial or a bottle
in the room.   Miss Sheridan had come at once and called
his name once or twice.   Then she said, " Get a doctor, Mrs.
Groves, get him quickly.   I don't know what can have
happened."

" She looked," said Mrs. Groves picturesquely, " like
Lot's wife, the one that was turned to salt, only this time it
was more like stone."   Dr. Wales had come along about
twenty minutes later, said Richard was dead, and started
asking questions.   When he spoke about a post-mortem
Miss Sheridan exclaimed, " But—what could it have
been ? He was never ill in his life."   No—in reply to a
question from the coroner—he'd never been one for taking
medicines or pills or anything and Miss Sheridan the same.
She'd told the police about the glass she'd washed, well, it's
what anyone would have done. Empty glasses standing around
got broken . . . She couldn't, of course, say when the beer
had been drunk.   He might have had it before he went out.
The house would be empty at the time . . .

Alison Sheridan was an elegant haggard figure of about
fifty.   She was dressed with her usual neatness in a hand-
tailored suit of chestnut brown with a minute black fleck ;

she wore a black hat and shoes and carried an enormous black handbag. The effect was as striking as if she'd turned up swathed in crape.

She agreed that Richard was her dead brother's only child, whom she had brought up since his third year. Both parents had been killed in an air-raid in 1944. She said he had always had excellent health and so far as she knew he was in no kind of trouble. She realised he was in love with Hatty Savage but she hadn't expected them to get married, at all events not at present. They were often out together and at one time they'd seen a great deal of each other ; she had warned him not to bank too much on that.

" Why did you say that, Miss Sheridan ? "

" Hatty Savage is the daughter of a very rich man. My nephew was employed in the bank. I didn't suppose Mr. Savage would look very kindly on an engagement, not, that is, until Richard had made more headway." No, she knew nothing of any financial troubles, he out-ran his salary occasionally and she came to his rescue but only for comparatively small sums. He was very anxious to have a car of his own, but she didn't consider he could afford to run one on what he earned. He was very popular and always got a lift with someone. He was inclined to be extravagant, but then he was young. He'd never given her any serious trouble. No, he hadn't spoken of wanting to live by himself ; she had hoped he might come into the restaurant, but he didn't fancy the idea. He had always been easy-going, when he was a small child she had had some evacuees for two years or so and they had all got on very well. When he was five years old she had given up the evacuees and got a job in a factory and he had gone to school. She had begun to work at The Clover House about ten years previously, and five years ago she had bought the lease and the goodwill. Richard was twenty-one and six months. No, he hadn't said anything about proposing to Hatty Savage, but he had seemed a bit tensed up, as she put it, at breakfast that morning. " I shan't be back till late," he said, " don't wait up, but I might have some news for you." No, she hadn't associated that with Miss Savage, she had wondered if perhaps he had been promised promotion at the bank. She hadn't heard him come in, she had come back from the shop later than usual and, being tired, had gone straight up to her room. So she couldn't help about the beer glass either. She had apparatus for making tea upstairs, and she had gone to sleep almost at once as she always did. Richard must have come in very quietly, she didn't even hear his door close. The first thing she knew about his being back at all was Mrs. Groves coming in and telling her there was something wrong.

"You knew your nephew very well, Miss Sheridan. Did he ever give you the impression that he was likely to take his own life ? "

"Never. Why should he ? He was popular and young, and if he really hadn't cared about his work at the bank he could have taken up something else."

"Do you think that if he had suffered a romantic setback it might turn his thoughts to suicide ? "

"I'm sure it wouldn't."

"If the means to accomplish it suddenly became available——"

But she shook her neat, shapely head. "I can't believe it. He was affectionate, he'd realise what it would mean to me. Besides, at his age life's very sweet and he had so much to look forward to . . ."

That was all she had to say.

Hatty replaced her in the witness-box and repeated the story she had already told Ferrers. The effect on the court was electrifying. As her answers accumulated, the very atmosphere seemed to thicken, like a fog. Alison began to rock a little where she sat, as if some machinery were beginning to work. The woman next to her held her arm.

"There, dear," she said. "There."

The coroner barely concealed his sense of outrage.

"You wish us to understand, Miss Savage, that, knowing this young man was in an excitable state of mind, greatly disappointed by your refusal of his offer of marriage, and at the end of an evening when no doubt he had drunk a fair amount of spirits, you deliberately handed him the means of taking his own life? Is that really what we are to understand?"

"If he hadn't meant to kill himself it wouldn't have mattered what I gave him," Hatty defended herself, "and if his mind was made up he'd have done it without me. Why, he hadn't even any guarantee that the pills were anything but aspirins, they look quite like them."

"But you had told him that three would be a fatal dose?"

"Yes."

"And you gave him three?"

"Yes. But of course I never dreamed he'd take them. Some people commit suicide but he wasn't the type, and anyway he hadn't got enough reason."

"He had just proposed marriage and you had refused him."

"I didn't even take him seriously, he wasn't in a position to marry anyone. I thought it was some kind of crazy joke. I mean, he didn't even suggest getting engaged. He said, 'Let's elope, then nobody can stop us.' As if I'd do a thing like that to my family."

"But now you do agree he was probably in earnest?"

"I don't know. He was such an actor, he ought to have gone on the stage, talking about being made use of—if anyone was made use of it was me. He couldn't have had half so much fun if he hadn't had lifts and invitations—and then pretending he only came because I was there . . ."

Cobb tried to stop her but it was no use. On and on she went like a river in full spate, the words coming quick and fast like water rushing over the edge of a rock, sweeping everything with it, leaves, twigs, all the flotsam and jetsam of months. Henrietta sat beside her husband, her hand clenched in his till her rings cut into her fingers.

"Can't anyone stop her?" she muttered in an agony. "She's terrified, and we can't help. And other people will think she doesn't care."

The coroner waited for her to run down. Then he said quite kindly, "I am sure the jury will appreciate that Miss Savage has had a great mental shock. I am afraid I must ask you some more questions in order to try and determine this young man's state of mind. You were in his confidence ? "

Hatty ·recovered some of her earlier calm. " If you mean did I know of any other kind of trouble he was in that might lead him to commit suicide, no, I don't. It was only when he said that about getting married secretly I began to wonder . . ." she hesitated.

" Yes, Miss Savage."

" I began to wonder if perhaps it was John Savage's daughter he wanted and not just me."

Alison's voice could be heard ejaculating " Infamous ! " Her neighbour whispered to her soothingly.

" Did you make it clear you intended the break to be a final one ? "

" It's so difficult to remember exactly what either of us said. I do remember saying I wouldn't marry him if he had ten thousand a year. I—I was a bit het up myself by that time. I dare say we both said rather more than we meant. And really what I wanted most of all was for him to get out of the car before he upset us both."

Cobb found himself thinking, " What's she concealing ? And can she go on ? Why was she so afraid ? "

She was followed in the witness-box by a man called Turner, the barman at the night club, the King of Hearts. He said he remembered the young lady coming in about twenty minutes before closing time, his licence expired at 2 a.m. She had had a young man with her, he had seen the deceased and could identify him as the party in question. They had both seemed a bit—keyed-up, the young man particularly so. He had talked rather loudly—more boisterous really, said Turner, knitting his brows in a passionate effort to find the right word. Richard Sheridan had left the bar for a moment and the lady had ordered the drinks. A double dry Martini—make it dynamite, she had said, he remembered that particularly—and a gin and tonic. She had made him fill her glass to the brim with the tonic, saying that she had to drive and it was getting dark, would probably rain. He had no sooner brought the drinks than two more late customers came in and he went to serve them. He hadn't heard Hatty's conversation with her companion, he was getting ready to close down; he had not found any empty phial on the premises after they had gone. This last piece of information was in reply to a question from the coroner, clearly at the instigation of the police, and it transformed the situation. Because now the dullest of the jurymen was compelled to realise that everything depended on the word of the girl who was the central figure of the affair. The young man was dead, half-way to the cemetery already, they'd hardly remember his name a month hence, but Hatty was in the very middle of the stage, with all the spotlight playing upon her. And they reminded themselves and, later, one another, that everything depended on her version of what had happened. If Richard could have told his story, if Alison had been awake on his return and had heard his side of it, how different might things appear? Thanks to Mrs. Groves's assiduity in washing the beer glass it was impossible now to prove whether the stuff had been taken in that final drink or had been dropped, during Richard's absence, into the "dynamite" cocktail at the King of Hearts.

The members of the jury exchanged doubtful glances. Cobb told himself they couldn't bring in an adverse verdict, there'd have to be a motive for murder. And who was going to produce that?

The next instant he had his answer.

There was a small commotion in the back of the room and a girl struggled to her feet; she was a stranger to them all, small and round in build, almost kittenish, with air hair springing childishly from under a round woollen cap.

"I must insist," the coroner began, but she broke in. "I want to give evidence. I knew him better than she did, and I know he didn't commit suicide."

She gave her name as Marguerite Grey and her occupation as a saleswoman in the glove department of Bootles, the big multiple dress store at Brightling. She had been there nearly five months, and it was there that she had met Richard Sheridan. He had come in to buy a pair of gloves for his aunt's birthday.

"And from that first meeting," she said, "we knew we had something that would bind us together all our lives."

Alison winced at the phrase and the rapt manner in which it was spoken, but the rest of the court was absorbed.

"We were going to get married," Marguerite went on. "That's why I know what Miss Savage says can't be true, that he was urging her to go away with him. Because we were engaged. Oh, I hadn't got a ring, I know, he said we must wait a little before announcing it. He didn't mean to stop on in the bank, he had a plan, and as soon as he could find the propitious moment—that was his actual expression —he was going to take me to meet his aunt. I never thought we'd meet under these conditions," she added, her voice shaking a little.

Her appearance, of course, changed the whole situation. Cobb wasn't certain at first whether it was helpful to his client or not. Suppose the gossips were right who believed that Hatty had been in love with the dead youth, and he had admitted his preference for this Marguerite Grey, might she have given him the deadly drink by way of revenge? If I can't have you, no one shall. Melodramatic, certainly, but it was his experience that melodrama is by no means confined to fiction. Or—Hatty might have found out about Marguerite and given the young man the go-by. Then when he went into his act about putting a bullet through his brain, she could have given him the tablets in the contemptuous anger of which everyone knew she was capable, and he might actually have taken them. Philip Cobb knew a good deal more about Hatty than any of her family realised. He knew that both she and Richard Sheridan were capable of behaviour that to him would be impossible, but all the same he couldn't see Richard meekly taking the pills and not even leaving a note to implicate the girl. But Marguerite's appearance did explain why he might urge Hatty to elope with him. Once married, there was nothing Marguerite could do about it. It was thoroughly unsatisfactory, look at it in any way you pleased. Everything depended on the unsupported word of the various witnesses. And, as any policeman (and Arthur Crook) could tell you, unsupported evidence doesn't get you very far.

He looked thoughtfully at the jury. He could see that this new development had tilted the scales sharply against the dead man, who now appeared as a heartless young opportunist, playing hard to win the rich girl and having his bit of fun with the poor one. For it appeared he hadn't spoken of Marguerite to anyone, not to his aunt, his colleagues or, so far as evidence went, to Hatty herself. Alison, recalled, gave testimony to this effect. " I hope," she said bitterly, as she turned to leave the witness-box, " they're both satisfied now. They wouldn't leave him alone living, and now they've done their best to smirch his memory."

Not a doubt about it, the feeling of the court was with her.

There were a few other witnesses, mainly called in the hope of showing Richard might have had some reason for taking his own life. But he had spoken of suicide to no one, nor had he seemed depressed or agitated in any way. He was in no kind of financial trouble, he wasn't precisely a hard worker but he had made no secret of the fact that he didn't intend to make the bank his life-work, he had dropped hints of a plan of which he gave no details. One young man, who had occupied the next desk to him, roused a little excitement, when he testified, " Richard said, ' I've got her there, my boy, and she knows it,' " at the same time closing his fist like someone crushing a butterfly or a moth. But this witness couldn't put a name to the mysterious " her " and you could choose whether he had been referring to Hatty or Marguerite. On the whole the betting was on Hatty.

Philip Cobb wondered that her own family shouldn't have noticed she'd changed allegiances during the past weeks. He wondered a bit about the other fellow. He himself wasn't, of course, a member of the golden circle in which these young people moved, but he had his own reasons for knowing what was happening where Hatty was concerned, ana he had noted this London chap for whom, he believed, she would even have tossed her cap over the windmill. He hadn't surfaced, and he wasn't sure whether that was a good thing or no. His existence might prove a motive for Hatty wanting Richard out of the way. The young chap wasn't above a bit of blackmail, Philip thought. On the other hand, he could have supported the girl's claim that she never had any intention of marrying Richard Sheridan. Looking at Hatty's locked face, Cobb found himself wondering whether there had been any communication between the two, and if he was the sort to stand by a girl whose name was all over the front page of *The Daily Liar*.

And, as he had anticipated, the jury played safe. They brought in a verdict of death from barbiturate poisoning but insufficient evidence to show how the tablets had been taken. A thoroughly unsatisfactory verdict from everyone's point of view, but, he supposed, an inevitable one. People could go on speculating until the nine days' wonder was past, telling one another that Richard might have taken his own life, Hatty might have poisoned him, he might have taken the stuff not believing it was a fatal dose or not believing it was poisonous at all. Neither his character nor Hatty's was cleared, and the case couldn't be regarded as closed. If fresh evidence ever came up the police could start all over again. Nobody had found the empty phial and it was improbable now that anyone would. You couldn't ignore the possibility that Richard had tilted the tablets into his palm and pitched the phial away on the triangle of waste-land at the corner of Allen Lane, where Hatty had set him down. The place was a tangle of blackberry stems and brambles and a thrifty bird might have picked it up; or there was a deep, muddy little stream running along the by-road there, and the phial could have been tumbled and swilled along that. And when all's said and done one phial is remarkably like another.

So, with no one satisfied, the court rose.

Hatty drove back from the inquest with her father. " Sit well back in the car," he told her. " And don't be surprised if there are inimical demonstrations."

It was wise of him to drive her himself; he was held in great respect, people liked and admired him ; moreover, he was as strong as a bull and as staunch as steel. Only a fool would get into his bad books ; he had more power than it is nowadays thought suitable for one man to possess, and nobody doubted that he would spare no effort to break the man or woman who turned against his only child. Nevertheless, John himself was grateful when they reached home without mishap.

" What did you suppose would happen ? " Hatty asked him, as they came into the hall. He saw with a secret admiration that though she was very pale she hadn't batted an eyelid.

" Someone might have thrown a stone," he said.

" At me ? " Her amazement seemed genuine enough.

" Well, not at me." (Henrietta had slipped out of court earlier and gone home alone.)

" You might have expected them to show a little sympathy," declared Hatty with a downrightness that took him aback. " Of course people are sorry for Miss Sheridan, but I don't believe she told all she knew—about helping him financially, I mean. I don't suppose he paid anything to live at home, but he certainly wasn't the saving kind. And at least he's out of it all. Whereas I'm first accused of egging him on, and then it comes out in the most public way that all the time he was carrying on with a girl in a shop."

" He never mentioned her name to you ? "

" Never. And of course it doesn't have to be true. She looks just the kind that imagines, if a man holds her hand, he'll dash out in the morning and buy an engagement ring. You know," she turned into the drawing-room, where Henrietta sat waiting to pour the boiling water on to the leaves, " I can't believe he ever meant to marry her. He was much too ambitious for that."

As though the household had not had sufficient shocks for one day Philip Cobb dropped a bomb into their midst when he came round to see John Savage that night.

" It's as good a verdict as we could hope for," he told him bluntly. " Once Turner had gone into the box things began to look sticky. Still, there isn't a shred of evidence against your daughter . . ."

" If I hear of anyone even suggesting she is in any way responsible for young Sheridan's death I shall take action," John said violently.

" No, Mr. Savage, you'll just copy the deaf adder. There's no proof anywhere in a story like that. Everyone knows they haven't got all the facts."

" And they hold Hatty responsible ? What an illogical attitude. As if she could tell them anything she hasn't told them in court."

" As to that," said Philip bluntly, " we don't know. I was on tenterhooks in case some unexpected motive turned up. If anyone could have shown that your daughter had a particular reason to be afraid of young Sheridan . . ."

" What harm do you suggest he could have done ? "

" A girl like Hatty doesn't go unnoticed long," said Cobb slowly. " She and Sheridan were a bit conspicuous for a time, even in Brightling their names were coupled. Then more or less overnight she cooled off, which could only mean one of two things. She'd learned something about Sheridan that intimidated her, or she fell in love with some-one else."

John Savage called himself a democrat, but he felt a sense of outrage at this young man—he was thirty-two but it was young to John—so coolly discussing Hatty's situation. His manner had changed, he wasn't simply the lawyer employed to watch an employer's interests, he was talking man to man. He continued, " What plans has she for the immediate future ? " and Savage replied more coldly than before, " We hope she's going to join my wife's sister in London during the next day or two. She usually goes to Paris about this time of year, and Hatty likes Paris ; she has friends there . . ."

" And of course Richard Sheridan won't cut much ice over the Channel, particularly now he's dead." And then he said, " You might give her a word of advice, Mr. Savage. For the next few weeks she'd do well not to be seen around with this fellow, Duke. That's the kind of thing that wakes sleeping dogs and just till the storm dies down they're much better left to lie."

John said sharply, " No one has suggested that my daughter is responsible for Richard Sheridan's death," and Cobb replied with great aplomb, " Oh, come, Mr. Savage, you know that's not so. The jury didn't bring in an adverse verdict because there was insufficient evidence, but the case isn't closed, and there's no sense flying in the face of the man—and particularly the woman—in the street. If there'd been any evidence to show that Hatty had reason to fear young Sheridan, if he had possessed some secret, if there'd been letters that could have been produced . . ."

" In short, you're suggesting they'd been having an affair."

" I'm not suggesting it, but then it's different for me. I'm in love with your daughter, Mr. Savage, have been from the first time I met her at your house. I haven't said anything to date, because I knew I hadn't got a chance, but now things have changed and she might find a husband useful. I don't propose to worry her yet, take advantage of her situation, but it's only fair you should know I'm in the running, and I shan't stop until she's married someone else."

John Savage had never paid a lot of attention to him; Arbuthnot spoke well of the fellow, but until to-night it occurred to John he hadn't even known if the young lawyer was married or not. And here he was putting in for Hatty. He sounds a better proposition than this chap, Duke, John discovered to his amazement. A trier, a don't-know-when-I'm-beaten chap. If Hatty ever looked in that direction she'd have to mind her p's and q's, but they needn't any of them bother because, naturally, she never would. She'd go to Paris with Lady Dane and by the time she came back public attention would have been distracted to a later scandal.

" Go away ? " said Hatty. " Of course I shan't. Everyone would say you both believed I'd poisoned Richard and wouldn't have me in the house. Remember Constance Kent ? "

" Constance Kent happened to be guilty," said John.

" Don't be a fool, Hatty. You're not going to like being pointed at and whispered about and seeing your picture in the local Press. Your mother's rung your aunt . . ."

" Then she can ring her again," said Hatty. " I'm like Robert Browning—ever a fighter, so one fight more . . ."

" What are we to do ? " demanded Henrietta. " She must be persuaded to go."

" I shouldn't bother," said John heavily. " Give her a week's respite and she'll be only too glad to shake the dust of Burlham off her feet."

CHAPTER III

DURING THAT FATEFUL week Hatty stayed at home. She sat by the telephone, she watched for the postman. Now and again the telephone rang and she sprang to answer it, but it was never the call she anticipated. She ran to get the letters from the mail-box at the first click of the gate. To Henrietta these signs were unmistakable. It was equally obvious that no call and no letter was the one for which she waited so hungrily.

If the man of mystery didn't write other people did. The anonymous letters started arriving within twenty-four hours , of the verdict. They conformed to the normal pattern, a scrawl of filth in unrecognisable handwriting on cheap paper in cheap envelopes. The postmarks were mostly local, though one or two envelopes bore no stamps, were thrown over the gate and picked up in the garden. Most of them were the products of illiterate minds, but here and there an intelligence, hideously warped no doubt, but capable of sustained argument, was clearly at work. " Let me open all your post," Henrietta said, but at once Hatty flushed rosily.

" Of course not. They're not all anonymous letters. I still have friends."

" The obvious anonymous ones, then."

" You can't tell. Some of them are neatly typewritten. It's all right, it's only lunatics. They might be grateful to me giving them a field day."

Besides the letters there were the anonymous telephone calls. " Is that Lady Macbeth ? " a voice would inquire. " I wonder if you could spare me some of those sleeping-tablets." " I want to poison my husband," said a woman's voice, " and I'd like expert advice. You know all about it, don't you ? " And some of these, too, were sheer senseless obscenity.

Hatty went defiantly down to the police station on the fourth day but Ferrers told her her best course was to take no notice. " We can't trace this kind of thing," he said, " not when it's just directed against one person. If it was a kind of poison pen epidemic now . . . But all they want is for us to pay attention to them. Just put the envelopes on the fire. It'll soon die down."

" So you'll do nothing ? " The angry colour flooded her cheeks. She looked quite sensational.

" It's in your best interests, Miss Savage. These people only want some limelight, they'd like nothing better than for us to start making inquiries. You're just incidental," he added.

On her way home someone threw a stone in Hatty's direction. She whirled round but there were only two little boys playing assiduously in the gutter. She realised that if she so much as questioned them their mothers would be round at the Savage house within the hour ; anyway, you couldn't proceed against children, but her blood chilled to realise that even they had been drawn into the conspiracy. Certainly they were too young to read newspapers or attend an inquest, they were simply following the example of their elders.

No one from the Savage household went to Richard's funeral. Henrietta sent a wreath bearing their address but no name ; and Philip Cobb attended as John's representative. The girl, Marguerite Grey, had apparently got time off, for she was there, clad in black which deprived her of all colour and gave even her fair hair a greenish tinge. Hatty sat at her window · and watched the passers-by send flying glances upwards. She thought of none of them, she didn't even think much about Richard, she only wondered about the letter that didn't arrive and tormented herself with the fear that something had happened to the one who should have written it.

To Henrietta at this time she was quite impossible. " How do we know what really happened ? " she demanded furiously. " We've got the evidence we were given on oath. What's that worth ? The coroner made a great deal of the fact that there wasn't a letter and suicides always leave letters. But suppose there was and Alison destroyed it ? Oh, yes, she might, there's no limit to what Alison would do."

" If Richard had left a letter saying he was committing suicide on your account, I think you over-estimate Alison if you suppose she'd want to protect you."

" Of course she wouldn't want to protect me, she wouldn't want to protect anyone but Richard. Or there could be some other reason."

" This girl ? "

" I don't know. Why should he kill himself for her ? Unless she knew something about him."

" Such as ? "

" I don't know. Or Alison might have found the phial and thrown it away so as to save him from the stigma of suicide. Really, Mother, I begin to think it would be better if I'd been openly accused, then my enemies would have had to come into the open and I should have had an opportunity to clear the air."

Henrietta reported this conversation to her husband. " She'd have got a Not Guilty verdict, I don't doubt," John agreed. " But girls like Hatty don't realise the gulf that yawns between Not Guilty and Innocent, and not many courts can ensure the latter."

It was Mrs. Addison who drove in the last nail. Hatty telephoned to say she would be coming round to the clinic as usual the following day ; she had missed the previous week—we felt until after the funeral it might look unsympathetic.

" I can't imagine what you're thinking about, Hatty," exclaimed Mrs. Addison in sharp tones. " You can't come round here, not yet anyway. Pamela will take the notes— Oh, I'm not saying a word against you, I think you've been most unfortunate, but you know what the mothers are like. Your coming would disrupt the clinic."

Hatty began to laugh ; she laughed till she thought she'd suffocate. Henrietta, hearing her, came in and shook her into some sort of control.

" Did you know I'm a mass murderess ? " Hatty inquired. " It's not enough that I poisoned Richard, now they're convinced I've got a plan to smother all the children at the clinic. If I so much as show my nose in the waiting-room it'll have the same effect as the Black Plague. Mother, is it always going to be like this ? People not wanting to see me, not writing or ringing up . . ."

" They'll expect you to want to keep to yourself for a bit," said Henrietta. She also had been a little shocked at the reactions of " the Set." " Hatty, do see sense, go to your Aunt Evelyn."

" All right," said Hatty, suddenly giving way. " I expect that's the best thing to do. Unless she's afraid of having such a dangerous influence roaming at large through her flat."

Philip Cobb encountered Hatty in the street before her departure. " Just send for me if there's anything I can do for you," he offered.

" Such as ? " Hatty inquired, and was dumbfounded when he asked her to marry him.

" It's conceivable you might find a husband an advantage."

" You must be mad," said Hatty. " Don't you know what happened to the last man who proposed marriage to me ? "

" Oh, they say lightning never strikes twice in the same place," he told her calmly.

" But you hardly know me."

" What you mean is you hardly know me."

She considered.

" Does it occur to you I might marry you as a sort of refuge? "

" Just so long as you do marry me."

" And have your wife pointed at as one of the lucky ones ? "

" I think I can promise to look after my wife."

He seemed more like a being from another world than the one she knew so well. She couldn't visualise marriage to such a man. Besides, she was in love in a quite different direction, and all at once a look of such tenderness and hope passed over her face as struck him to the heart. He knew then she was thinking of a secret lover whose name bore no analogy to that of Philip Cobb. But he thought the chap must be a pretty poor type, staying under-water like a skulking submarine, and the time would come when she'd see him in his true colours—yellow as the dawn—and that might be his opportunity. For that he was prepared to wait.

Hatty put him out of mind almost at once. It had occurred to her that London should be a possible place to contact Alan Duke.

Evelyn Dane received her niece with an outspoken, " Well, Hatty, this is a pretty kettle of fish. You can't learn too soon there's never any sense counting on men behaving in a reasonable way. The reasonable thing would have been for young Sheridan to have thrown the tablets back in your face and I dare say that's what you expected."

" Oh, Aunt Evelyn," cried the girl, " do we have to talk about Richard all the time ? I can't open a letter or lift a receiver without someone telling me I'm a murderer. The idea of coming to London was to get into a different milieu. Father's a very important man in Burlham but surely up here . . ."

" People like John Savage are important everywhere, and don't make too little of that, Hatty. It's probably helped you more than you know during this last week. How soon will you be ready to come to Paris ? "

" I thought it might be nice to spend a few days in London," Hatty urged. " Then next week say . . ."

Evelyn rang up her brother that night. " Hatty looks very strained," she said, " and no wonder. But she'll get over it. Don't write to her a lot and don't expect to hear from her. Once we're in Paris things will assume a more reasonable perspective."

In the circumstances her aunt had not arranged a very lively programme for her. " It'll be all right once we're across the Channel," she promised, " but your father's daughter can't get into this sort of pickle and remain unnoticed."

She was going out to lunch on the second day of Hatty's visit and asked the girl if she could entertain herself. " Ask anyone in you like," she offered.

" I'll go out to a restaurant, I think," said Hatty, looking better already for the change. " I'll ring up a friend and see if we can meet." As soon as she was sure her aunt was off the premises, she put on a very smart new hat and went out to the telephone box in the mews round the corner. She knew, of course, their line wasn't being tapped and there was no one in the flat to eavesdrop, the morning woman having just departed, but she was taking no chance of interruptions. She was lucky enough to find the booth untenanted and she dialled a Hampstead number. When she heard Alan Duke's voice answer she half swooned with joy, drawing long breaths as though she had been suffocating for days and days.

The young man at the other end spoke twice before she could find her voice.

" Who is it ? Duke here."

She spoke very low as though she were afraid the whole world was listening in.

" Oh, Alan, it's Hatty."

" Hatty ? Hatty Savage ? " A new note sharpened the easy-going voice.

This was the very thing he had feared, but as the days went on and she made no move in his direction he had begun to think Fate was going to let him off for once. He wasn't without dash himself, but marrying a girl who might already have put one unwelcome suitor out of the way was the act of a lunatic.

The soft, eager voice was speaking again. "Well, how many Hattys do you know?"

"Where are you speaking from?" he compelled himself to ask.

"At the moment I'm in a call-box off Curzon Square. I'm staying with my aunt, she talks of taking me to Paris."

He pulled himself together. It mightn't be as bad as he feared.

"Lucky Paris. Lucky you, come to that. My old dad used to say that to be young and in Paris is to dwell in Paradise."

"I'm not your old dad," Hatty pointed out, and her voice had changed, become fuller, more gay and assured. "Oh, Alan, I've been in such a stew. Why didn't you write? But I suppose," she added, with a humility quite new to her, "you were afraid they might open my letters or something."

"Good lord!" He sounded indignant. "Do they usually?"

"Because of the anonymous ones. They've been pretty horrible."

"You poor sweet! I'm sure you're wise to flee to Paris, get out of the limelight for a bit."

"I kept hoping you'd telephone or—or something."

"Hatty sweet, do have some sense. What sort of a verdict would you have got if it had been generally recognised there was another chap in the picture? I was only thinking of you."

"Yes, of course. I didn't sound as if I blamed you, did I? Alan, I must see you. Where can we meet? Could I come to your studio? I've always longed to see a real artist's studio."

"Good lord, no, darling." His voice came like a streak of light. "You'd compromise me to death. Besides," he added quickly, "you'd want to start tidying up. Women always do, goodness knows why. The world's untidy enough and we artists are supposed to hold a mirror up to life. Let me think. How long are you in London ? "

" Well, Aunt Evelyn's going to Paris early next week."

" And this is Friday ? "

" Yes. She's gone out to lunch, she won't be back till about six. They're taking in a matinée or something," she added vaguely. " So I'm free for hours and hours."

He thought quickly. " Too bad, I've got to meet a chap about a commission. What's the time now ? Just gone twelve. Look, do you know the Blue Grotto ? "

" A taxi can find it if I can't."

" Meet me there for a quick drink. I'll have the glasses set up by the time you arrive."

She was left holding the receiver in her hand ; hearing the familiar buzz that indicated her contact had hung up. She replaced her receiver thoughtfully, and a large woman in a mackintosh, though there wasn't a cloud in the sky, and carrying a basket that was apparently full of fish, thrust past her into the box. She walked through Curzon Square into Raymond Place, where all the spring flowers were beginning to shine in the window-boxes and half the parked cars had uniformed chauffeurs standing guard over them. She crossed by the little garden square off Prout Street, and saw the proud ladies with their shaven poodles and shaggy schnauzers making their way home to lunch. It was strange to be in a place where no one noticed her and no head turned.

She reached the Blue Grotto before Alan Duke, and idly ordered herself a dry Martini. She was sipping this and looking round when Duke came in, looking like a golden hoop bowled by the wind. He bowled himself up to her table and stopped dead.

" What's that ? A Martini ? I will say for you, Hatty, you've got spirit. Mind you, you're quite right." He hooked a chair forward with one foot and sat down. " Don't let people crush you. Aren't you dying to go to Paris ? "

" I don't know. I'd just as soon stay in London."

" Hatty ! The girl's crazy." He called a waiter and asked for a double whisky and soda. " And another of those things, Hatty ? Right. Good lord, how far away Burlham seems."

" It's my home.· Mother was going to ask you to her next Cold Comfort party, but, of course, everything's been cancelled. It's funny, Richard didn't seem anyone of particular importance when he was alive, now he's dead he seems to condition everyone's affairs."

" Neurotic sort of chap," said Alan Duke. " Must have been. Look, Hatty, sweet, you're not going to let this spoil things for you ? God knows it's a ghastly thing to have happened, but no one could really hold you responsible."

" That's nonsense. Heaps of people do."

" Oh, well, they don't really count. And at least it's got you out of that place."

" Only temporarily. I was rather an embarrassment to my family. And, of course, Miss Sheridan hated me."

" Poor old girl! I don't think I met her, did I ? Do you think you may stay in Paris for a time ? It might be quite a good idea. You've got good French, haven't you ? I seem to remember the night we went to that French place you were jabbering away like a frog yourself. Do stay in Paris, Hatty, I could come and see you."

" You could come and see me in Burlham," she suggested.

" Yes—well." Some of his gaiety fell from him. " You know how they gossip in a little place. Besides, there's really very little to do. Now, Paris—funny thing, I was thinking of going over anyway. You've been before, of course ? "

" Of course."

" Then you know people there. Oh, come, Hatty, you can't mean you'd sooner stay in Burlham ? I should think it was a bit awkward now. For your father, I mean."

" I don't necessarily have to stay in his house."

" Then who—good lord, not Miss Sheridan ? "

" Of course not. She'd like to see me hanged, drawn and quartered. No—Philip Cobb—did you meet him ? (Alan shook his head). He wants me to marry him."

" Stout feller ! Are you going to take him ? I mean," he added, aware of his own clumsiness, " one does like to hear of chaps who don't let a bit of gossip or scandal put them off. What's his line ? "

" He's a lawyer." Her voice was levelling out, the peaks of pleasure flattening.

" Never any harm marrying a lawyer, those boys know all the ropes. Did I meet him ? "

" I shouldn't think so. He's not exactly a gay proposition."

" All got to settle down sometime, old girl. You do like the fellow, I suppose ? " he added, as though the thought had only just occurred to him.

" I don't know him very well."

" He must be a good chap, though."

The sun that had been shining when she entered the Blue Grotto appeared to have gone in ; a sort of darkness seemed spreading over the land.

" Could I have another drink ? "

" Of course. You're like the people in the hymn I used to hear my father sing—did you know I was a parson's son ? Oh, yes, they always make the best rakes, they say— who tremble shivering on the brink and fear to launch away. Botheration, where's that waiter ? Never mind, I'll get 'em."

" No," she said quickly, " this is my round. I'll get them."

" Never heard such rot. No, Hatty, I mean it. O.K., we'll wait till the fellow comes." He glanced at the natty little gold watch on his wrist. " Take their time here, don't they ? "

" Why didn't you write ? " Hatty asked abruptly as they waited. Something in her voice shrieked a warning.

All his gaiety and élan vanished, as if someone had passed a duster over a blackboard.

" Hatty—for God's sake, what was there to write about ? Here ! " He had caught the waiter at last and given the order. " What *was* there to write about ? " he repeated as the man moved off.

" People generally send sympathy in a case of bereavement."

" Honest, Hatty, you'll have me round the bend. I thought you didn't even like the chap much."

" Life isn't the only thing you can lose. There's reputation and friends and . . ."

"Look, let's not go all melodramatic and tragic over this. Of course, I'm sorry for Sheridan, but the fellow was obviously a fool and not worth your losing your beauty sleep for. If he hadn't got the stuff from you he'd have got it from somewhere else."

She said desperately, "What did you think when you heard the news ? When did you hear ? Was it in the London papers ? I didn't read the papers just then."

" Oh, they gave you a lovely press, darling," he assured her.

" That's something to be grateful for, isn't it ? " said Hatty. " I mean, it almost makes it worth Richard dying, doesn't it ? And everybody had a lovely read."

He put his hand quellingly over hers. "Do look out," he said. " People are starting to look."

" Why shouldn't they ? " demanded the girl, suddenly brilliant. (Oh, definitely more than half round the bend, if you asked him, unless she'd been filling up before his arrival.) " Aren't I worth looking at ? Of course, if the jury had brought in a different verdict I'd be even more of a draw, only then, of course, I wouldn't be here at all."

He wished to goodness she wasn't. Couldn't she see this affair had changed everything ? Hatty Savage, daughter of a rich tycoon and pretty as they come, was one thing ; a girl who conceivably might have murdered an inconvenient lover was quite a different cup of tea. And, suppose she had done it (and no one but herself would ever be sure) there was no saying she wouldn't try again. *C'est toujours le premier pas qui coûte*, as our brothers over the water liked to say. The first step—once you'd taken that and it hadn't landed you in a quagmire, you might easily try again. Thank goodness he wasn't actually committed. The thing now was to get her away as quickly as possible before some infernal press chap jumped up, disguised as a cocktail shaker, and started snapping his little box, and there in the evening editions Mimi (an inveterate reader of newspapers) saw them both and started throwing the book at him. After all, it was bad luck for her in a way, Sheridan turning out a bad hat, but a fellow had to look after himself, and he didn't want to be tagged for the rest of his days as the man who married that girl who gave her lover a dish of cold pizen— no, a cup. He turned to find Hatty regarding him with a perfectly mad glance.

"Why wouldn't you let me get the drinks just now?" she was asking. "No, don't tell me. I know. You thought I might have some more of those little tablets handy—and how do you know you weren't right? Look!" She snapped open her bag and took out a tiny gold box that John Savage had hung on last year's Christmas tree. "It's called a patch-box, and it's the perfect size for pills." She opened it as she spoke, and he saw them, four little white tablets. "Actually, they're aspirin, but I don't suppose you believe that." She put one in her mouth. "Does that convince you?"

"Do you want the whole place staring at you?" he said again.

"You're frightened," she taunted him. "You're yellow. That's why you left me to go through that all alone. I couldn't believe it at first. I said, he's bound to come when he hears I'm in trouble. He'll tell them we're in love, so why should I want to do Richard any harm? And you didn't come. You don't know what it was like, standing there, everybody staring, being questioned, knowing people were saying, of course she slept with him, and he threatened to make trouble . . ."

People were looking now all right, but most of the glances were envious ones. At any time it was difficult to overlook Hatty. Her kind of beauty isn't to be met every day of the week. Hardly a man in that room didn't yearn towards her, the older ones recalling with a pang their own youth, and the golden girls who had vanished with the golden summers that were barely a memory now.

"Look," he implored, "you've had a bad time, I know. Later on you'll see it was all for the best that I didn't butt

in. Don't you see, I'd have provided your motive for—
for——"

" Poisoning Richard ? "

" For God's sake, keep your voice down. Here come the
drinks at last."

She asked casually; " What does it feel like to be drunk,
dead, insensible ? I'm sure you know. Would you recom-
mend it ? "

" I'm going to take you back to your aunt," he said
abruptly. " Have you seen a doctor ? "

" I don't need one. I'd sooner have another of those."
She swallowed her drink in two swift gulps. " That was
good. I shall love Martinis my whole life long, as Swinburne
very nearly said."

" Good God, she's right over the edge," thought Duke,
pale with embarrassment. He managed to get her to her
feet and out on to the pavement. The cynosure, he thought,
of every eye. Outside the air blew cool and rainy ; he looked
round distractedly for a taxi.

" We might walk," said Hatty, but he wasn't having any
of that, quite capable of trying to put herself under a bus,
and then turn and accuse him of attempted murder without
a qualm. The commissionaire saw them and came up
smartly.

" Taxi, sir ? " One was just drawing up to disgorge
passengers. Alan Duke stood impatiently on one side, still
clutching her. " You do look passionate," Hatty whispered
tauntingly in his ear ; he looked sheer murder, but he
pushed her inside the cab, then realised he didn't know the
address.

" I can't remember your aunt's number," he said with
an effort of friendly deception for the driver's benefit.

Hatty—that beastly girl—wouldn't play ball. " I never
gave it you. I rang from a call-box—remember ? "

" I mean, her number in Curzon Square."

He was convinced everybody thought she was drunk.
But he turned to the driver. " The young lady's a little
faint, she's not been well. Take us to Curzon Square and
. . ."

"Number twelve," said Hatty in a cool voice. "It's all right, she won't be there."

"You mean, there's no one else in the house?"

"It's a flat. Well, I shouldn't think there would be. But I'll be all right. Why not? It's not when you're by yourself that you're in danger."

By this time she really had very little notion of what she was saying. In her extremity she had summoned up a kind of robot who took over and used her voice, borrowed her gestures.

Alan Duke would have given a week's pay to let her go home alone, but in her present mood there was no knowing what she mightn't do, and there'd been scandal enough already. They drove in silence to Curzon Square and when they arrived she said, "Don't bother about seeing me in, I've got a latch-key."

The porter, hearing a taxi draw up, came to open the door. Hatty stepped out and walked away without a backward glance. Alan said, "That young lady, I don't know who she is, she seems to have been taken sick or something. I brought her back—is there anyone to look after her? She said something about an aunt . . ."

"Lady Dane is out at the moment, but I'll go up and see if there's anything I can do." He looked expectantly at the young man. A woman on the pavement stopped to inquire, "Is this cab free?" and Alan said, "No, no, I'm going right back." He plunged his hand into his pocket, brought out a coin and pressed it into Masters's palm. Then he said, "The Caprice," and was driven quickly away. If he had looked back he might have seen Masters staring with incredulous disgust at the penny embedded in his palm.

"The Caprice," said a voice in his ear and he realised he'd arrived. He bounded out, his heart a deal lighter than it had been an hour before. He'd seen the last of Hatty Savage and he hoped to heaven she'd go to Paris and stay there till the cows came home.

A handsome woman was fuming in the bar. "I gave you a watch for your last birthday, Alan," she said.

"And very good time it keeps. Now, no scowls, darling,

they don't become you. Something very important came up . . ."

"Something in a mink coat?" But she was smiling already. Hatty wasn't the only one who had found him irresistible.

Lady Dane came in at half past three.

"How did your lunch date go?" she asked.

"Oh, wasn't it a shame? I got there a bit early and I'd just ordered a drink when suddenly I felt quite faint and a man at the next table insisted on getting a taxi and bringing me back here. Wasn't it kind of him?"

"Press?" asked Evelyn Dane alertly. Really, you couldn't expect to have a face like that, that had been in the papers so recently, and not be recognised.

"No. Oh no, I don't think so. I suppose he was sorry for me. And Masters insisted on giving me two of his wife's Aspros and he brought up some chicken cocotte. So you see you don't have to worry about me."

The shadows under her eyes were as blue as a wood at twilight; Lady Dane knew she hadn't heard all the truth, but she had the sense to know that sometimes it's smart to stay ignorant. She began to talk about Paris. "You won't believe me now," she said, "but in six months' time none of this will seem real."

"It doesn't seem real now," said Hatty, politely. "Perhaps actresses feel like this."

Suddenly she hungered for Paris, the strange, the enchanting city, where she had been a student for a year and where, if anywhere, she could disembarrass herself of this wretched shadow, Hatty Savage, and start all over again.

CHAPTER IV

RICHARD SHERIDAN had been buried a week. In her house, empty and cold as a shell, Alison Sheridan sat with her hands folded in her lap. An immense silence surrounded her. It was Sunday, when The Clover House closed at three o'clock. Not even the radio had been turned on. She sat in a stupor so deep that it was some minutes before she became aware that outside the window life stirred. Someone on her doorstep was ringing the bell. She sat like a stone. The press, she thought. For some days after the tragedy they had dogged her path, wanting statements, asking questions, even invading the restaurant. The bell rang and rang. Then the knocker rose and fell, but still she didn't stir. When, however, a hand tapped insistent as a bird at her window-pane, fury suddenly moved within her. She rose and tore back the curtain, then paused aghast. In the frail evening light she saw a face framed against the pane. The cheeks appeared greenish but the wide-open eyes stared straight into hers. It was the girl, Marguerite Grey.

"What do you want?" she whispered, forgetful of the barrier that separated them.

The girl gestured. "Go away," said Alison. But the face remained pressed against the pane. Like a sleep-walker, Alison got up and went into the hall. She opened the door and Marguerite came in like a ghost, like a shadow.

"I thought you were going to let me freeze to death there," she said reproachfully.

"You don't freeze to death in five minutes."

"I'd been there much longer than that. At first I was afraid to ring."

"Why did you come anyway?"

"It's not my first visit," Marguerite explained. "I've been twice before but each time you were out."

"I work late," said Alison mechanically.

" You won't need to work so hard, though, now. Will you ? "

" Why not ? Nothing's changed so far as The Clover House is concerned. Except that now I'm alone."

" That's what I came about. You could feel rather like a fish in an outsize pool in this big house. Are you thinking of letting it go ? "

" I don't know. I haven't had time to consider."

" On the other hand, it's not easy to find a new place, and this is beautiful. You must be very fond of it. Richard used to say——"

" Is that why you came ? To talk about Richard ? "

" Of course."

" I haven't anything to say. Richard's dead."

" Do you feel him near you ? "

Alison made a gesture of intolerable strain. " I can't talk about him."

" I think you should. At least to me. Other people are different."

" Other people knew him much longer than you did," said Alison brutally.

" But perhaps not so well." In the same tone she added, " I've lost my job. At least I gave it up. Deane said he couldn't have the newspapers always calling. Did they come here ? "

" What do you suppose ? "

" You'd be at The Clover House, though."

" They deduced that too."

" It's queer, isn't it ? " She settled back more comfortably, linking her hands round her knees. " While he was alive no one paid a lot of attention to him. He liked attention, didn't he ? It's a pity he can't see what a furore he's creating now he's dead. I wonder if he thinks it worthwhile—dying, I mean."

" Now you're talking nonsense. Miss Grey, why did you come ? "

" Couldn't you call me Marguerite ? I'm almost one of the family."

" I don't know what you mean by that."

" I must have seen you in the old days, I mean when I was quite small. We lived at Fishers End."

Alison looked dumbfounded. " Did Richard know that ? "

" Oh, yes. I must have seen him when he was a little boy."

" There were so many little boys. Why should you remember him? I must ask you again—why are you here ? "

" I thought you might be lonely."

" I shall get used to it."

" You don't have to."

" What do you mean by that ? "

" I was wondering—would you like me to come here— for a time anyway ? "

" Here ? But—what on earth could you do ? "

" I like looking after houses. I could look after yours."

" Mrs. Groves and I——" Alison began.

The smooth white brow furrowed. " I'm not sure you're wise to trust her as much as you do. She's a gossip, you know. Down at the Duck and Green Peas every evening. And I'm not even convinced she's honest."

" Don't you realise that's a very dangerous thing to say ? Actionable in law. Unless, of course, you've proof——"

The huge green eyes flew open. " But I'm only saying it to you. We oughtn't to have any secrets between us——"

" My dear Miss Grey ! "

" Oh, you must call me Marguerite. After all, if he hadn't been poisoned I should have been his wife."

" Then, Marguerite, we'd best indulge in a little plain speaking. Richard never mentioned you to me."

" He knew you'd set your heart on his marrying that girl, Hatty Savage. I suppose it could have been a lift-up for him, a clerk in her father's bank, but whatever she may say he never gave her another thought after he met me. And of course she was jealous, that's why she killed him."

" There's no proof——"

" I'll get it. What's the matter, Miss Sheridan ? Don't you want her to be brought to book ? I don't mean to leave a stone unturned. Oh, I know she's a rich man's daughter, she's got all the advantages, but that won't save her. And I shall need all my free time to get my evidence, so it's a good thing really I had to give up my job."

She spoke so calmly, with such a tranquil assurance, that Alison felt herself being hypnotised.

" I think you're making a great mistake," she heard herself say, " and I really don't need anyone living here with me."

" But I've got to live somewhere and my landlady's like Mr. Deane. She doesn't like reporters, she says they get the house a bad name: and she says her sister's girl is starting work in Brightling next week and has asked Mrs. Pond to keep an eye on her and mine's the only suitable room in the house. She probably hasn't got a sister and if she has I don't suppose the sister's got a girl, but I can't prove that and Brightling's always packed, it's frightfully hard to find anywhere to live and you've got this big house here—who does the furniture belong to ? "

" It's mine, of course."

" It's lovely, isn't it ? It must have cost a lot of money. I've never had any furniture of my own, just what they call utility and even that wasn't mine. Richard always said you had very good taste. It's easy to see that to you a table isn't just something you eat off. That's a lovely vase."

She strolled across the room and lifted it from its bracket.

" Be careful," breathed Alison instinctively. " I brought that back from Italy."

" I've never been abroad. I'd love to go. I suppose you used to take Richard. Perhaps next time——"

" Now, Marguerite, you know this is all a pipe-dream." But the girl could discern desperation under the calm voice. " There's no question of our setting up house together. We're strangers—you and I——"

" We shouldn't be strangers long living under the same roof. I'm a good cook—did you know ? "

" I'm not needing a cook."

" Not at the moment but no one can foresee the future, can they ? We couldn't have dreamed this would happen to Richard. I dare say I could be a lot of help to you in your restaurant. I've always thought I'd like to have a stake in a business." She put the vase back. " Did you buy all this furniture ? "

" Most of it. A little came from my mother."

" Didn't any of it belong to Richard's people ? "

" I thought you knew. They were killed by a bomb during a night raid. The house was demolished."

" But you must have bought some of it with the money his father left you. I wonder why he left it to you and not to his son."

" Richard was three years old at the time and it was a condition of my brother's will that I should make a home for his son until he was sixteen."

" I know. He told me. He went to Somerset House, you know, to see the will after he was twenty-one and got the letter his father had left for him. It must be strange to get a letter from someone who's been dead eighteen years."

" Quite a number of men who knew they might be killed left letters for their sons. It's quite natural. You wouldn't want to be quite forgotten."

" Do you believe in immortality, Miss Sheridan ? Or may I call you Aunt Alison ?"

" I'm not your aunt."

" If I'd married Richard——"

" I still shouldn't have been your aunt. And you must face the fact that you weren't even engaged."

" I suppose you believe what that awful girl said at the inquest. It wasn't true, of course. He never wanted her to elope with him. People think he wanted her money, but why should he? He'd got you, and your business is doing very well, isn't it ? But you'll want a partner some time."

" I'm going to put the kettle on for a cup of tea," said Alison, abruptly coming to her feet. She felt like someone under a spell, she the masterful, the ruthless even, when occasion demanded, as inefficient employees could testify. She didn't want this strange girl here, had no intention of having her. For all her apparent softness and consideration, her kittenishness, little round face, fair fluffy hair and small dimpled paws folded so meekly on her knee, she gave out an aura of implacable strength.

When she came back with the tea-tray she found Marguerite sitting just where she had left her.

"There's one thing I didn't make clear," said the girl, lifting those limpid green eyes. "I don't mean to be a charge on you. I've got Richard's hundred pounds."

"Richard's hundred pounds?" The tray trembled in her hands. "What on earth are you talking about?"

"Didn't he tell you? The bonus he got from the bank at Christmas, it was to be the foundation of our bank account. That's why he gave it to me. He said money slipped through his fingers. Oh dear, you've forgotten the sugar. I'm afraid I'm a great sweet-tooth. It's bad for the figure, I know, but Richard said he didn't like skinny girls."

"Did he tell you the hundred pounds was a bonus?" Alison poured out a cup of tea and handed it across the table.

"Of course. Why should there be any secret about it?"

"Banks don't pay their junior clerks bonuses of a hundred pounds."

The lids fell captivatingly over the big green eyes. Marguerite sighed. "That's what he told me. Perhaps she gave it him."

"She?"

"Hatty Savage."

"Why on earth should she?"

"I don't know. You might ask her."

"Do you realise what you're suggesting?"

"Well, anyway, wherever he got it from he gave it to me."

"Perhaps it was an advance of salary. Though I must say it doesn't sound like John Savage. And why did he give it to you?"

"I told you. He wanted us to start a bank account."

"I could have saved it for him."

"Perhaps he was afraid of your asking where it came from. Middle-aged people are so old-fashioned, about money particularly. Why shouldn't she give it him?"

"There's only one reason why a girl in Hatty Savage's position gives a young man money and that's in answer to a

threat. If you're suggesting my nephew was a blackmailer
——"

Marguerite leaned forward and put a small confiding
hand on her companion's knee.

"You don't have to keep up appearances with me, Aunt
Alison," she said simply. "We both of us know what
Richard was. Only—provided we work together there's no
reason why anyone else should know."

A few minutes later she stood up to leave. "That tea
was quite nice without sugar," she said in surprised tones.
"I can see you're going to be a very good influence for me.
I'll move in next week and it would be nice if I had Richard's
room. I'm sure when you think it over you'll see it's the
best idea."

After she had gone Alison sat for a long time with her
head in her hands. When at length she moved it was with
extreme caution as though she knew she was face to face
with a blank wall and couldn't batter her way through.

Twenty-four hours later Alison went to see John Savage
at his bank. The sight of her in daylight away from her
hotel was startling. What she had to say was more startling
still. Although on the surface she was her usual trim,
elegant figure, he found himself thinking: this is a desperate
woman.

"There's something I want to ask you, John," she said,
coming to the point at once. "I know it's unorthodox but
you and Henrietta have always been good friends to us."

He thought: it's money, and so it was, though not in the
way he had anticipated.

"It's about Richard. You must tell me. Is it your practice
to give your clerks a bonus at Christmas?"

"I'm afraid not." John looked puzzled. "Has anyone
suggested——?"

"I knew that wasn't true. Well, then, did Richard ever
ask for an advance on his salary?"

"I doubt if he'd have got it if he had. But in fact he
never did. What's all this leading up to, Alison?"

"He had a hundred pounds," she said slowly. "He had
it in notes—at least it was notes he gave her."

" Gave whom ? "

" Marguerite Grey, of course." She seemed amazed that he should need to ask.

" Has she bobbed up again ? Why on earth should Richard be giving her a hundred pounds ? "

" I think she had some hold over him," said Alison carefully. " She says he gave it to her to save against their marriage."

" Do you believe her ? "

" I believe she was a danger to him."

" Well, she can't harm him now. Unless—you don't mean——"

" I don't think he was having an affair with her, if that's what you mean. John, you don't think Hatty could have given him the money ? "

" I don't believe Hatty ever owned as much as a hundred pounds at one time."

" She could have borrowed it. With you for security—"

" But why, Alison ? Why ? Are you suggesting Richard had some hold over Hatty—— ? "

" No. No, I suppose not. But this girl's out to make trouble for us all—beginning with me."

" She can't do you any harm."

" You haven't heard her suggestion."

John listened. " But that's preposterous," he exploded when Alison had come to a dead stop. " She can't fasten on you like—like a leech. You've only to say you don't want her——"

" It sounds so simple, doesn't it, and I probably should say just the same if it were you. But—she means to come."

" You said she knew something about Richard. Have you any idea what ? "

" I only know it was enough for him to give her a hundred pounds."

" Is there any proof he did ? "

" Someone did. She showed me the notes. I even looked through my own cheque-book. When people are desperate they act entirely out of character—but there are none missing——"

" You didn't seriously think——"

" I begin to feel Richard is a stranger to me. Suppose he'd known something about someone that was worth a hundred pounds——"

" In that case why should he have taken the fatal dose ? It's the victim who does that——"

The same thought flashed through both their minds. John couldn't bring himself to voice it, but she had more courage.

" John, what happened to that phial Hatty says she gave him ? It wasn't in the house."

" Either it was overlooked or Richard threw it away."

" It wasn't overlooked. We all searched. And why should he have thrown it away ? Where is Hatty ? "

" In Paris."

" She's lucky. You can't shut your eyes to the fact that Marguerite Grey is going to be a danger to her, too. She's said as much."

He looked at her compassionately ; he and Henrietta had known her for some years, had admired her drive and enterprise. He had seen her sometimes pacifying difficult customers, never giving way to her real feelings. A superb actress, he had thought. Unshaken, unshakable. But the mask was off now. She had joined the short list of those who were afraid, because Richard Sheridan had died and no one could be certain how it had come about.

" If there was any real motive why he should have taken them," she said desperately. " I must ask this, there was no trouble at the bank ? "

" No. Everything was as straight as a parallel line. It wouldn't surprise me if your Miss Grey isn't at the root of the trouble. Alison, I implore you, don't take her into your house."

" She wouldn't be any less dangerous because she was under another roof."

" How can she be dangerous ? "

" She had some kind of a hold over Richard."

John put his big strong hand over hers. " What kind of a hold, Alison ? "

Gently she drew her hand away. " You're a parent, John,

you know how they feel. Richard was like my own son to me. You'd defend Hatty, wouldn't you, through thick and thin, whatever she did . . ."

" You're not suggesting she was responsible for Richard's death ? "

" She's bound to be partly responsible; she gave him the tablets. Did she say anything to you about him ? "

John had a vision of his daughter crying to Henrietta, " I wouldn't have married him for all the tea in China." Aloud he said, " Richard's gone, Alison. Nothing this girl does or says can hurt him now. Don't let her prey on you."

Alison began to draw on her soft French kid gloves. " Suppose it was Hatty ? Would you let people, strangers, throw mud at her just because she wasn't here to defend herself ? "

" I doubt if many people would listen."

" I doubt if you've quite got our Miss Grey's measure. On the whole, it's better to have her where I can see what she's up to. I never liked the notion of people striking from the dark."

" If she makes trouble," John suggested, " you could go to the police."

" It's not that kind of trouble. Don't forget what I said about warning Hatty. This girl considers she's been cheated out of her birthright—that's her melodramatic way of putting it—and she doesn't care who she hurts to get even."

Within a fortnight of her arrival at Star Cottage Marguerite Grey had dislodged Mrs. Groves. " As good as told me I was light-fingered," stormed the charwoman to her cronies in the Duck and Green Peas. " You mark my words, Miss Sheridan's going to rue the day she took that viper into her bosom. No better than she should be, if you ask me, and it wouldn't be surprising if Richard took that stuff to get away from her. 'Who do you think's going to keep this place clean ?' I asked her. And the way she looked down that little snub nose of hers—I could have taken her over my knee. 'That's my work,' she said. 'That's why we shan't be needing you any more.' We. I told her, 'It's

news to me this house belongs to anyone but Miss Sheridan.'
' Oh, there'll be plenty of changes,' she said as bold as brass.
' This is only the start.' "

Now when Alison came back in the evening she found the
house ablaze with light. " I like light," Marguerite told her.
" There's so much darkness in the world, don't you agree ? "

" I went to Curtis to-day," said Marguerite a few nights
later. Curtis was the exclusive dress shop patronised by
Alison, who had never entered Bootles except to buy a
packet of pins or a needlebook. " You have an account
there."

" Well ? " Alison's tone was chilling as frost.

" I need a new dress."

" I'm sure they'd welcome you as a customer."

" I thought you might tell them it would be all right to
put it on your account."

" Surely," said Alison sarcastically, " you don't intend to
desert Bootles."

There was a moment's silence. Then, " You shouldn't
have said that," Marguerite told her quietly. " You can't
afford to insult me. I've only got to tell other people what
I know about Richard. Don't forget I've got proof."

Burlham talked, of course. " She seems to have adopted
that Grey creature," the matrons gossiped to one another
over cups of coffee at The Baker's Dozen, pots of tea at the
Copper Kettle.

" According to her, she was engaged to Richard."

" According to *her* ! "

" You'd wonder Miss Sheridan puts up with it."

Then Alison lost a waitress at a busy time and Marguerite
donned an apron and filled the gap.

" Of course I don't mind," she said in response to Alison's
protests. " You mustn't think I'm too proud. Besides, I
like to see how you run the place."

" It's very odd you shouldn't have a car," she suggested
a week later. " Richard always thought so."

" I can't drive a car," countered Alison, grimly.

" You could learn. Or I could learn and drive you. I wish
you'd stop thinking of me as an enemy. Actually, you know,

I'm your best friend. Why, if I wasn't, do you think I'd have kept quiet so long ? When's that Hatty Savage coming back ? " she added in the same breath.

" Why not ask Mrs. Savage ? "

" I dare say she doesn't know. Not that I blame her. In her place I wouldn't dare show my face in Burlham again. She must know the Sheridan case isn't closed. If any fresh evidence came to light she could still be tried for murder."

" I shouldn't advise you to say that kind of thing openly. John Savage would make a bad enemy. Try and realise that."

" It might be a better idea if you were to warn Hatty Savage I'd be a bad enemy, too. She's bound to be coming back sometime and she'd find me much more useful on her side. You might tell her that if you get the chance."

But in the event Alison had no such opportunity. When Evelyn Dane returned to London she left Hatty in Paris. Three months later Philip Cobb, on holiday in that queen of cities, tracked her down, overwhelmed her defences and married her out of hand. The news in a picture paper of Alan Duke's marriage to a wealthy widow, first name Mimi, might have had something to do with the decision. For there's no sense in love ; at any time, had he called her, she would have gone, and since she couldn't have him, why not be reasonable and take what's left on the plate ? She tried to explain this to Philip—" I don't want to marry you under false pretences," she said—but he looked bland as he answered, " Ah, but I'm getting the only thing I wanted. And you don't have to worry about a reception committee when we get back. For one thing, you'll be Mrs. Philip Cobb, a person of much less speculation than Hatty Savage, and for another, I like to think I'm able to look after my own wife."

She looked at him standing there, staunch as the Rock of Gibraltar, but the Rock would be a hard thing to bang up against. She gave a faint shiver. This wasn't how she had imagined it would be. She had visualised a white wedding with everyone there, hosts of presents, the Voice that breath'd, champagne corks popping and in her heart all the bells of the world a-chime. And the reality—a private, probably rather drab ceremony at the Mairie, with strangers for witnesses. One or two of her French acquaintances might attend to see her " turned off," as one of them had wittily remarked the previous week—to this had beautiful, envied, happy Hatty Savage come. And there were plenty who'd tell her she was lucky to get a husband at all and a house in Bridge Street, Brightling, and the companionship of his colleagues' wives, all older than herself.

" But why ? " she cried. Why, she meant, does this have to happen to me ?

He misunderstood her. " I thought I'd made that clear. Because I love you."

" Most people would think you crazy, but if that's what you really want . . . Love ! " she repeated softly, in the tone of one who knows all about it and knows it's nothing but a rotten joke.

" Well, it's called the divine madness, isn't it ? 'I attempt from love's sickness to fly.' Who said that ? Only some of us are natural hypochondriacs who hope they'll never be cured."

CHAPTER V

ON THE DAY that Henrietta received her daughter's letter telling her that she had that morning married Philip Cobb in Paris, she found herself outside The Clover House in Brightling. On an impulse she pushed open the door, reminding herself she must have lunch somewhere. It was almost two o'clock and most of the lunchers had departed. Henrietta took an empty table and ordered the onion soup for which the place was famous, with a Spanish omelette to follow. She had just finished the soup when Alison appeared. Henrietta's heart jumped ; she was as elegant and trim as always, but there was something there, a haunted look, fear, an emotion one didn't normally associate with that prim perfection, that almost took Henrietta's breath away. Alison went round the few occupied tables making sure that customers were satisfied ; it pleased them to feel themselves singled out and if there were complaints she could consider them later. She reached Henrietta's table almost before she realised who she was. But recovering herself, she asked, " Is everything all right ? "

" Need you ask ? " returned Henrietta. " Of course not. Oh, not the food, that's always perfect. But—how tired you look. People of our age shouldn't be subjected to this long stress of emotion. Sit down, Alison, and have a glass of wine. Yes, of course you can. At this hour of the day the restaurant runs itself."

Alison capitulated ; she called the waitress. " Mary, bring a half-bottle of the Chambois '53. This is on the house, Henrietta. Yes, of course it is. I can still afford to buy my friends a glass of wine."

Henrietta was shocked by the haggard desperation of her manner ; she remembered what John had said after her visit to the bank three months earlier. " Like a free creature discovering it's caged. I tell you, Henrietta, I was shocked. We haven't heard the last of Richard's death by a long chalk." The wine came and was poured out.

" I wanted to tell you about Hatty," Henrietta said.

" Is she coming home ? "

" Not home, not to us, that is. She's married Philip Cobb."

Alison looked as though nothing could ever surprise her again. " Oh, well," she said with a faint shrug. " I suppose it's one way out." And she added, " Are you pleased ? "

" It's hardly what either of us had anticipated for her," Henrietta answered. " I did think she might settle in France for a bit, put the past behind her."

" That's what she should have done." Alison's voice was harsh with fatigue. " What on earth made her marry a man ten years her senior whom she hardly knows ? Don't tell me she's in love with him."

" Perhaps he spells security for her, the only security

she can find now. Alison, does it sometimes seem to you none of it's worth while? It's all a cracking bad joke? Think of our hopes for our children——"

" No," said Alison in the same harsh voice. " Don't think about the past at all. Hatty's started a new life. Your world and Mrs. Cobb's will hardly impinge at all. If she's any sense she'll leave Hatty Savage behind her in the grave, with Richard——"

For a moment it seemed as if she would break down but Henrietta's hand came out, cool and strong, to hold hers.

" Well, this is going to annoy Marguerite," Alison observed. She gave a ghost of a chuckle.

" Marguerite? "

" Miss Grey, No, she's not here any more. She found she hadn't got a vocation to be a waitress. Besides, she was an upsetting influence. Henrietta, you should warn Hatty that girl's her implacable enemy. If she can do her a mischief, she will. I warned John three months ago."

" I wouldn't give much for Marguerite Grey's chances against Philip Cobb," returned Henrietta in scornful tones.

" At one time you might have said—I certainly would have said—you wouldn't give much for her chances against me—but I'd have been wrong."

" Alison, my dear, Miss Grey can't hope to injure Hatty more than she has been injured already."

Alison said nothing, and Henrietta went on rather hurriedly, " How long is she staying at the cottage, by the way? "

" Oh, she's quite settled down, I gather."

" But—why do you have her? Why can't you tell her to go? "

" I can't. I told John, didn't he pass the information on? She knows something I wouldn't have made public for the world."

" Something about Richard? "

" Yes, you could say that."

Henrietta considered. " I shouldn't presume to advise you, Alison, you've made such a success of your life. But why should this girl be a danger to Hatty? "

"Can't you realise that she holds Hatty responsible for Richard's death? Mind you, I don't believe she was really in love with him, but he represented her first chance of getting away from the glove counter. She's older than she'll allow, I'm certain. And you can't escape from the fact that Hatty gave Richard the tablets that killed him." Her voice hardened. "There's no sense not facing facts."

"If Hatty doesn't recognise that by this time there's no hope for her," said Hatty's mother in controlled tones. "Tell me, Alison, have you ever seen an anonymous letter?"

"Why do you ask that?" demanded Alison quickly.

Henrietta looked surprised. "I never had, till Hatty started getting them. Why, Alison, surely no one wrote to you?"

"Not this time, no. But more than sixteen years ago I had my share. Sixteen years is a long time, but one doesn't forget."

"*You* had them? Alison, I beg your pardon, I didn't intend to pry . . ."

"It's all right," said her friend listlessly. "In fact, I've sometimes wished I could talk to someone, just to be reassured . . ."

Absently she picked up her empty glass, then set it down again. "You know that saying, old sins have long shadows. Well, I suppose it wasn't a sin precisely, an accident—it would be blasphemous to call it an Act of God—it was something no one could have foreseen or, in fact, prevented, which is why it seems so very hard that I should be faced with a bill all these years later."

Henrietta had never seen her friend like this, Alison, the sturdy, the indomitable.

"Tell me if you can," she said gently, "that is, if you'd like to. I don't want you to feel I'm forcing your confidence."

Alison signalled to the waitress and ordered coffee. "Two black," she said, "and two liqueur brandies. Oh, yes, Henrietta, you will, just this once. It's something I haven't mentioned to anyone for years," she said, "something I never meant to talk about again."

" And this girl, Marguerite Grey, is involved ? "

" No. At least, well, she's like a left-over from that time."

The coffee arrived and the brandy and the waitress withdrew. " Never try and understand the workings of Providence, Henrietta. One thing I've always appreciated so much about you and John is that you never ask questions, you don't pry. I never talked about my life before I came here. You know, of course, that under my brother's will I became Richard's guardian. Before the war I was an infant-school teacher—I wasn't very good and I didn't like it, but it was a safe job and I hadn't any particular qualifications. In those days I had no capital and I never thought of entering the hotel business on the bottom rung. I was involved in 1938 and again in 1939 in the mass evacuation of children from danger areas. Harry—my brother—said he couldn't leave his London job and Naomi wouldn't leave him, not even for the boy. They'd only been married three or four years. So I took a cottage—it was very remote but I thought it would be safe—and they sent Richard to me. I had three other evacuee children, all much of an age, a boy and two girls, and I taught them myself. I enjoyed that. It was the first time in my life I'd been independent. Mind you, I had to be very careful, the other three children were Government-sponsored evacuees and the pay was wretched, but at least I didn't have the parents as well. Little Dick Smith, the other boy, was one of those unfortunates, in a way it was lucky for him that he came to us. His mother was no good and any one of half a dozen men could have been his father. Of course, he'd never known any home life and she was only too anxious to be rid of her responsibility. Do you know in the two years or so that he was with me she never once came to see him or sent him a present, not even at Christmas ; she never sent any money for his clothes—why, I had a photograph done of him locally and sent it to her, it seemed so dreadful he should have no one and he was such a handsome little boy, I thought her heart must melt."

" But it didn't ? "

" She was either married by then or one of the unmarried

wives who got a marriage allowance from the War Office. She didn't acknowledge the picture though I know it got there, because otherwise it would have been returned. Of the little girls—one was an evacuee, the other was an orphan, she was adopted towards the end of the war, and I think she went to Canada as soon as it was over. Louie was plain, but a nice little thing. They all got on quite well, and I had a woman to help . . ."

" Alison, you're not trying to tell me Marguerite was one of the two girls ? "

" Oh, no. She's much older, she'll never see twenty-five again and it wouldn't surprise me to know she was more. If you watch her when she's thinking about something you can see she's not really young. But her parents lived at Fishers End, our nearest village, we used to do shopping there, and once a week I went into Leffingham on the bus to get the rations. We rubbed along all right. My woman who helped me got married but I got another. It was hard work, of course, but I didn't mind that. Then in 1944 Harry and Naomi were killed, and Richard really became my son. You know about the will. Harry made me his heir on the condition that I made a home for Richard. When he was sixteen I got the capital. Not that I needed any persuasion, I loved him for his own sake. It was the following year that it happened."

She picked up her little liqueur glass and drained the brandy at a gulp.

" It was market day, the day I always went into Leffingham. You remember what the war was like, Henrietta. You had to get your food at certain shops and give coupons, food stamps some people called them. That day for some reason Mrs. Long didn't turn up. She was as regular as clockwork and the only other time she'd been sick she'd sent a substitute. I didn't know what to do. I had to get the food, there wasn't enough in the house, the rations barely stretched the week as it was, I waited and waited—I didn't hear till afterwards that she'd been knocked down by an army jeep in the dark the night before and died in hospital next day without recovering consciousness—and at last I decided I must take a chance and go in on the twelve-thirty bus, whisk round and, if I could, get a taxi and come back in that. Only taxis were as hard to come by as eggs or fresh lemons . . . Richard was four and a half, they were all much of an age, Louie was the only one who'd turned five. It was warm weather so there were no fires, and I went round the house collecting every box of matches and locking it away. Afterwards people said it was criminal to leave four young children alone, but what would they have done, I'd like to know ? " Her voice rose stormily. " I couldn't let them starve, I couldn't take four young children with me on the bus, you had to stand as often as not. I put out their toys and a few sweets—there weren't many of those, I was buying a new supply in Leffingham—and off I went. I was as quick as I could be, but, as I feared, a taxi was out of the question, and the buses only ran once an hour. There was a war-time habit of closing the shops for the lunch hour and some of them stuck to it even on market day. Well, I got the absolute necessities and back I came. I was away about an hour and a half."

Alison picked up a piece of bread, crumbled it and let it fall.

" I was asked afterwards, at the inquest, if I hadn't felt anxious, but I could truthfully say no. I locked the back door, because if they strayed out into the woods they might have got lost, I locked up the step-ladder and I put the knives on a high shelf where they couldn't possibly reach them—and they were good children, didn't quarrel much and being four they could play together—you know how young children live in a world of their own. I managed to get a pound of dripping from the butcher off the ration, I was planning to make dripping toast for tea, that was a rarer treat than wedding cake—and when I came staggering down the lane, absolutely loaded with parcels the first thing I saw as I turned the corner was smoke pouring from the cottage's upper windows."

" Alison—how appalling."

" It was in the boys' room. The two little girls were on the landing, they were in tears but mostly I think because they were afraid of being scolded. They rushed at me and hampered my movements. I pushed them downstairs. 'Go into the front garden and stay there,' I said. They were both crying and one began to scream hysterically. I opened the door of the boys' room ; it was full of smoke. I was blinded for a moment. The fire had got a real hold by that time. I could make out one child lying on the floor by the door, so I grabbed him and pulled him out. I swear, Henrietta, I didn't know which one it was. It was only when I reached the hall I realised it was Richard. He was unconscious. I propped him up in the doorway and went back for the other one, but I couldn't get into the room. It's true, Henrietta, I couldn't get into the room. None of the children was old enough to use the telephone, but a passing van had seen the flames across the valley and came up to help. Richard was still unconscious and we could get no sense out of either of the girls. I remind myself sometimes what it must have been like doing rescue work in London during the raids, but I can't believe anything could be worse than what *I* endured that day."

" I never dreamed," murmured Henrietta, appalled. " But, Alison, surely you don't blame yourself. No one could have done more."

" You wouldn't have thought so if you'd heard the neighbourhood gossip afterwards. I always believe it was a Miss Lomas who started it ; she was one of these women who always wanted to marry and have children and she'd had a disappointing life. Then she applied for evacuees but the authorities didn't think her situation satisfactory."

" Started what ? " Henrietta inquired.

" The rumour that I deliberately saved Richard because he was my own blood, and let the other boy suffocate. It was nonsense. I tell you, until I was outside the room I didn't know which child I'd got. There was no sense leaving him in the passage, I had to get him down the stairs . . ."

" Relax, my dear." Henrietta laid her hand on her friend's arm. " I suppose there was an inquest ? "

" Fortunately that took place at Leffingham. Well, we

were just a pocket of existence, not more than about thirty
people all told, and Leffingham was our market town.
There was a tremendous shortage of doctors, and even
coroners were half a dozen other things. I wondered if it
would have been better if we'd had it where we were all
known, because then at least people would have realised I
had done my best for them. At Leffingham we were virtually
strangers."

" And the verdict ? "

" Death by misadventure. No one said anything, not a
word of censure, not officially, I mean . . ."

" Well, of course not, why should they ? "

" But all the same there was a general air of unease. So
convenient, they whispered, that I should have saved the
right child. There'd have been far more sympathy if I'd
brought little Dick out. And I've always thought it sinister
that the authorities decided to re-house Patricia—the pretty
one, the orphan—themselves, while Louie's parents arranged
to have her back. Anyway, after what had happened, I
couldn't have carried on. I kept Richard, of course, but we
never went back to the house. It was pretty well unin-
habitable anyway, thanks to the fire. Do you remember,
Henrietta, in the war how often something went wrong with
the water supply during the worst raids ? Or the hoses
weren't long enough or something ? There was a water
shortage that afternoon. I rescued a few things, but the rest
I bought as and when I could. I only wanted to guard
Richard against the gossip, so I took him right out of the
neighbourhood. He went to school a month or two later
and I took a job in a factory."

" How did the fire start ? " Henrietta inquired.

" Didn't I say ? The children got bored after a while
and started foraging in drawers and they found my cigarette
lighter and they carried it to the window and started flashing
it and set the curtains alight, and of course they were too
young to try and extinguish the flames before they got a
proper hold. I wake in the night even now sometimes,
thinking how terrified they must have been."

" I don't know," murmured Henrietta. " I don't believe

children have a great appreciation of danger. They probably thought the flames were wonderful."

" The girls at least had the sense to go on to the landing, or perhaps the boys drove them, I don't know, I never asked Richard much about it, I didn't want him to brood."

" You should have spoken of it before," said Henrietta compassionately. " You've nothing to blame yourself for, my dear . . .".

" I don't know," whispered Alison. " I simply don't know. I've thought about it so much that sometimes I wonder if the anonymous letter-writers had some basis for their accusations, that perhaps I did in my heart differentiate between the children, and . . ."

" You couldn't conceivably have distinguished them in a smoke-filled room. Did the relatives make a lot of trouble for you ? "

" I told you, there were none. Several of my correspondents commented on that. No doubt, they said, I had thought the child expendable . . . The doctor said he must have died of suffocation before the flames touched him."

" Do you think about it often ? " Henrietta asked.

" No," said Alison simply. " Sometimes I don't think of it for months at a time. Then there's something in the paper about a child being caught in a fire and it all comes rushing back. Henrietta, I've never said this to anyone, but if I'd known which boy was which and had realised I could only save one, do you think I'd have taken Richard ? "

" You shouldn't torment yourself," Henrietta warned her. " You still haven't explained where Miss Grey comes in."

" That was another chance, something I couldn't have foreseen. I go down to Leffingham once every year to see the grave, and put flowers there—he had no one else, you see—but this year for the first time I was prevented and Richard went in my place. And that's when he met Marguerite."

Henrietta looked startled. " I thought she told the court she met him at the glove counter at Bootles."

" That's what she told the court, but in fact she met him down there. She was in the churchyard putting flowers on her mother's grave, the old lady died about a year ago, and Richard asked her if she knew where our boy's grave was. They got talking and it seems she remembered the affair— I told you it attracted attention and she was just the age, about ten, I suppose, when that kind of thing sticks in the memory."

" Did Richard know the story ? "

" I hadn't gone into a lot of detail, he simply knew there was a child who died in an accident. He never asked many questions. Not till after that day. According to her, it was love at first sight, but that's wishful thinking. Richard was my nephew but I hadn't got too many illusions about him. He was very ambitious, he'd never have married anyone like Marguerite and she knew it. But she saw a chance to advantage herself . . . Why not ? "

For Henrietta was shaking her head. " She couldn't hope to resurrect the story after all these years."

" You don't know what those letters said, Henrietta. And the affair was fully reported in the local Press. Richard was a child then, but he's a man—was a man—when he met Marguerite. And it could do my business harm still, and it would have done Richard harm. You know how sensitive the young are, how convinced they become that they're objects of interest, of scrutiny, of conjecture. I didn't want him hurt either."

" But he's dead," said Henrietta, gently. " Alison, what are you really afraid of ? "

Alison lay back, her hands limp upon her knee. " I suppose I was a fool to hope to deceive you. Yes, of course there's more to it than that. She knows something about Richard I won't have made public even if he is beyond all harm, and she's malicious enough, for all her smooth ways, to make mischief just out of revenge. That's why I say tell Hatty to be careful. She may be in greater danger than she knows."

" I think Hatty's husband will be able to look after her. He's not exactly a weak-minded man."

" Richard wasn't exactly weak-minded, and he had me behind him, but she was too much for him."

" You mean, you really believe he committed suicide—deliberately ? "

" I didn't at first, but now—oh, yes, Henrietta, Richard killed himself, and I know why."

CHAPTER VI

LIKE A BUTTERFLY in the sunlight, or a moth after dusk, Marguerite Grey fluttered through the Burlham streets.

" Don't you get bored, having nothing to do all day ? " Alison inquired, and Marguerite opened her huge green eyes and repeated, " Bored ? Nothing ? But I haven't got nothing. I've got the cottage. And then people are so interesting. It's like sitting on the touch-line, watching the game, seeing the details the players don't notice."

She spoke in such a gentle voice, her lips curved into such an appealing smile, her glance said, " I know you think I'm silly, but I simply can't help it."

The intimidating manner she had adopted at their first meeting was gone now ; she wanted to help, she said, wanted to be made use of. " You could ask me anything," she would plead. " I just want to be part of a community, that's all."

Sometimes, lying in bed at night, Alison would find herself shivering. She had known the need to be a member of a community, someone who counted, she could still remember. Ambition was dangerous, and she was never under any illusion about Marguerite. It was like living with a virus. You could never be sure whom it would attack next.

Having cups of coffee in Brightling cafés, riding so demurely in the hourly buses, buying stamps at the post office-cum-drapers, Marguerite's eyes and ears served her like the antennæ of a butterfly ; she drank in sounds and sights, storing both in a phenomenal memory. Sometimes just for fun she would sidle up to some woman she had noticed meeting a man, obviously not a husband, perhaps at the market on a Wednesday, and offer some greeting. If the woman stared and said, " Aren't you making a mistake ? " up would go Marguerite's feathery pale-brown eyebrows.

" Oh, but you were at the market last week. I saw you with your husband."

" Oh," the woman would generally murmur, taken by surprise, " that wasn't my husband, just a friend . . ."

It was as easy as that. " Oh, silly me ! " Marguerite would say prettily. " Of course, I've never met Mr. Brown or Jones or whoever it might be. I'm Marguerite Grey, I live at Star Cottage with Miss Sheridan."

As if the whole neighbourhood didn't know her after her dramatic intervention at the Sheridan inquest !

" What's she after ? " the woman would think, feeling fear's hand on her arm.

Marguerite would laugh for sheer pleasure. Power was delicious. She wasn't making anything out of it, of course, but it was about time people realised she wasn't invisible.

One evening she turned into a narrow street in Burlham, and, passing one of the tiny houses it comprised, she heard someone singing, an odd jumble of words in a cracked old voice. The curtains had been rather carelessly drawn, and it was possible to look into the lighted room. Marguerite looked. An old woman sat on a sofa with a glass in her hand and a bottle on the table. As Marguerite watched, she refilled her glass. Like a witch, thought Marguerite. Mischievously she put out a hand and tapped the pane.

Instantly the old face turned, the dull eyes brightened, a shaking hand set down the glass, and the figure rose, a tall, emaciated old thing, moving unsteadily, but—" Born to the purple, I shouldn't wonder," reflected Marguerite. " You can always tell. Wonder what her story is."

A hand pulled the curtain imperiously back ; the two faces confronted each other—the young and soft, the old and disillusioned. Two thin hands came up and tugged at the sash. It moved a few inches and a voice croaked, " Who are you ? What do you want ? "

Marguerite walked through the gate and stood on the step.

" You called out," she said clearly. " Is something wrong ? Can I fetch anyone ? "

" Of course not. An absurd idea."

" Are you sure ? Would you like me to come in for a minute ? You don't look at all well."

" I am perfectly all right." The voice spaced the words with immense care. " I do not like being watched."

" I told you—you called out. Are you alone here ? Really, I do think—I mean, I feel responsible. You look as if you were going to faint. Do let me get you a doctor."

" I do not require a doctor. Will you please go away ? "

" Dr. Arnold lives on the corner. I'm Marguerite Grey, I live with Miss Sheridan. Oh, there's someone coming. Perhaps . . ." She half-turned. A moment later the front door opened, a hand came out and drew her within.

" We don't want to attract attention," said the agitated old voice. " Now, I dare say you mean well, but I don't need anyone."

It was a small room and the furniture was old and sound, without being really valuable. Victorian, decided Marguerite. There was a nice diamond ring on the old hand, no wedding ring, though. Disappointed in love and taken to the bottle, that was about the size of it.

" Now, Miss Havisham," she began.

" Havisham ? I don't know what you're talking about. My name is West. You've clearly come to the wrong house."

" I don't think so. I think Providence sent me here."

" What is it you want ? " panted old Miss West.

" I just want to help you. I haven't had a very easy life myself. I was going to marry Richard Sheridan, and then he died. Do let me put things straight for you."

She flitted about the room, shaking up cushions, straightening chairs. She smiled as she passed the bottle, but she didn't offer to touch it.

" You know." she said seriously, " if you were to apply to the local council I'm sure they'd get you a home help."

" I don't need anyone interfering. And I'm not alone in the world as you seem to imply. I have a nephew . . ."

Really, thought Marguerite, it was almost too easy. They handed you everything on a plate.

" Does he know ? " she asked.

" Know what ? " Panic whistled in the ancient voice.

" That you're alone and not well."

" I am perfectly well. I have said so three times."

" Don't *you* think perhaps Providence sent me here to-night ? I've never been down this little lane before. I get lonely sometimes with Miss Sheridan out all day, and I can't take a job because of looking after her house. Mind you, I'm not complaining, but people don't always appreciate . . . The charwoman she had was so jealous that she walked straight out as soon as I arrived. But I could come and see you sometimes, in the afternoons, perhaps I could do your shopping." Her photographic memory took in every detail of the room as she spoke ; she could have made a scale map of it when she got back. She was the kind of witness the police would never believe because she was too good to be true.

" My dear Miss Grey, that is most kind, but I assure you I manage very well."

" Everyone needs a little company sometimes. I could drop in and get your tea for you now and again. I'm sure your nephew would be relieved to know you weren't quite —well, uncared-for."

" My nephew is a family man with an important position. He lives in Hampshire. He really cannot be expected . . ."

" That's just what I say," broke in Marguerite eagerly. " I'm an orphan myself, my mother died a year or two ago. I still miss her very much. I should really like to come," she added. "Now, I'll drop in to-morrow afternoon just before four. Don't bother about tea, I'll bring you some home-made scones. I'm a very good cook. I wouldn't be surprised if one of these days I ended up cooking for The Clover House. Miss Sheridan will need a partner."

"Do you know an old woman, a Miss West, who lives in Beddoes Lane?" she asked Alison that night.

"I know of her. She doesn't go out much, prefers her own company, I understand."

"That's where you're so wrong." Marguerite clasped her little kittenish paws. "I met her quite by chance this evening. She's asked me to go to tea to-morrow. I thought I'd take some of my special scones."

"You're wasting your time," Alison warned her briefly.

"What do you mean?"

"She's got nothing for you. She's as poor as a church mouse."

"Oh, Aunt Alison." The soft, wounded voice matched the reproachful green eyes. "Don't you see, that's why? She's one of the people the world's by-passed, but she's still alive, though hardly anyone seems to realise it. And she's starving for a little companionship. I shall try and draw her out. There's no sense being dead till the clods fall on your coffin. Besides . . ."

"Well?"

"I'm afraid she drinks a bit."

"Why not, so long as she doesn't do anyone any harm?"

"If she wasn't lonely, she wouldn't need to drink. Aunt Alison, can't you ever credit me with a generous impulse?"

"My dear Marguerite," retorted Miss Sheridan, "I know you're *capable du tout*, but even you mustn't expect miracles."

Marguerite's real chance of making her mark came when Burlham decided to hold a fête in aid of refugees. They invited Brightling to join them, and got Henrietta Savage as chairman of the committee, which brought in Lady Martin from Grandison House, and a London office suggested a loan of a film, if they could guarantee a minimum attendance and would pay travelling costs, and someone proposed a tableau as well as the usual stalls, literature and refreshments. The idea caught on. For one thing, it made a nice change from the usual parish Jumble Sale for the preservation of

the Church Fabric Fund, for another there really was a lot
of feeling about these desperate people, and a corporate
effort is always easier, as well as being more entertaining
than just putting a postal order or a cheque into an envelope.

Marguerite dived head first into this opportunity. She
said gently that she could type a bit and she could help with
costumes, she was quite clever with her needle, and she
really wanted to help, not having had a home of her own for
a long time, which made her particularly sympathetic, and
she didn't mind what she did, they'd want someone to make
tea or wash china, and she could perhaps also represent
Alison, who simply couldn't give any personal service because
of her long hours at The Clover House.

Henrietta suggested to Hatty this might be her opportunity, but Hatty said at once she hadn't the time, and she
hated committees anyway. Henrietta sometimes wondered
how her lovely popular girl had turned into this pale, with-
drawn young woman, who didn't make the slightest effort
to re-establish contact with the people she'd once known.
Brightling was only about four miles from Burlham, but
they might almost have been in different counties. Hatty's
neighbours now were mostly the wives of the men Philip
Cobb knew, older than she for the most part, many absorbed
with young children. There had been some old-fashioned
looks when Philip brought her back as his bride, old Mr.
Arbuthnot going so far as to say it was the worst day's work
his partner had ever done.

"No one's going to flock round her," he said. And now
that people didn't pay afternoon calls and nearly everyone
had to do their own housework, invitations came slowly.
Hatty said she didn't care, she hadn't realised there were so
many bores to the square inch. She shot about the country
in her little white car and started a rock garden. John Savage
had made a generous marriage settlement, so she wasn't
short of money, but money hadn't the same value in her
new life. Henrietta had rather diffidently warned her
against Marguerite, and Hatty had replied indifferently, " I
can do a bit of warning too. Tell her to stay out of my way.
Not that I ever believed Richard meant to marry her ; he

was much too fond of butter. I suppose she was trying to entrap him into marriage and that's why he proposed to me that we should elope. That would have made him safe."

But she was reckoning without Marguerite. One afternoon, when arrangements for the fête were under way, someone rang the bell at 9 Bridge Street, and when Hatty opened the door there was Marguerite on the step.

" What do you want ? " she demanded inhospitably.

" Just a few words. Can't I come in ? I'm sure you'd rather we talked inside."

" I don't want to talk to you, inside or out."

" I think you will, when you know why I've come. I've got something of yours, you might like to have back."

" Something of mine ? " Hatty stiffened. " How could you ? Oh, all right." Like Miss West, she recognised that Marguerite had taken the first trick. " Come in."

Marguerite looked round interestedly. " Do you do all your own work ? "

" Why ? Are you wanting a job ? "

" Oh no." Marguerite laughed lightly. " I've got my work cut out at the cottage. And then I do quite a lot of voluntary work. I do enjoy that. By the way, that's one thing I did want to ask you—this refugee committee . . ."

" My mother has already asked me. I told her I was too busy."

" Perhaps I could persuade you to change your mind."

" You ? Of all people ! "

" Do we have to keep up this atmosphere of hostility ? " inquired Marguerite in plaintive tones. " After all, I haven't done you any harm, and if I'm prepared to be friends . . ."

" Why should we be friends ? "

" We both loved Richard with all our hearts."

" Speak for yourself."

" But you did, you know."

" Oh, nonsense ! Is that all you came to tell me ? "

" I told you, I've got something. You can't pretend now you weren't crazy over Richard . . ."

" Is that what he told you ? "

" It's what you wrote."

The blush that had risen to Hatty's cheeks at the mention of the dead youth was succeeded by a pallor so complete that anyone with a grain of compassion would have desisted. But Marguerite knew that nature's red in tooth and claw and we're all the children of nature, and there's no one to guard your interests except yourself, and she remained perfectly composed.

" I don't know what you mean," said Hatty at last.

" I know about putting the past behind you, but it doesn't cease to exist because you refuse to turn your head. Your letters to Richard . . ."

" There are no letters."

" Oh, but there are. You can't have forgotten writing them."

" Richard destroyed them long ago."

" Did he tell you that ? Because, if so, it isn't true. I've got them now, and very revealing they are. But, of course, you knew he hadn't burnt them. That's why he died. Because you wanted to marry this other man and if he'd read some of those letters . . ."

" What becomes of your statement that he was going to marry you ? "

Marguerite dropped her long lashes. " Oh, he was."

" Perhaps he hadn't realised that."

" How can we tell what he realised, now he's dead ? "

" That's why you came, of course. I realised . . ."

" I thought perhaps we could be friends."

" Oh, I see. You've come to offer me my letters in exchange for friendship. It's rather a tricky notion, isn't it ? "

" You don't change much, do you ? " sighed Marguerite. " You still think you're the one to name the terms."

Hatty looked outraged. " I hadn't mentioned terms."

Marguerite opened her bag. " They were quite wonderful letters, I was most impressed. I wonder if you remember what you said. No, don't try and snatch, this is only a copy. The originals are where you'll never find them."

Hatty shrugged. " What are you proposing to do with them ? Send them to my husband ? You don't know

Philip very well if you imagine he'd read letters not addressed to himself."

"Oh, I wasn't thinking of him. I mean, it would be a shame to waste them on someone who wouldn't even read them. But other people would be interested."

"Which other people?"

"The sort of people who read *The Sunday Spectacular*, say."

"They wouldn't risk publishing them. I could bring an action."

"I wonder. Anyway, would you? Hasn't there been enough publicity about you and Richard? Think of your husband if you won't think of yourself. It doesn't do a lawyer any good—and don't we hear Mr. Arbuthnot's thinking of retiring? Well, that's a great chance for Philip. He can't risk a blotted copy-book now."

"How much do you want for them?" asked Hatty abruptly.

"We-ell." Slyly Marguerite peeped through her long lashes. "I believe *The Sunday Spectacular* would give me something like a thousand pounds for them."

"Then why haven't you offered them already? You can't have hoped to get anything like that amount from me."

"Because money isn't everything, though, of course, it's important to have some. I like my position in society, such as it is, I'd like to be friends with you . . ."

"While you're blackmailing me?"

"Not blackmail." Marguerite remained perfectly unruffled. "I haven't demanded any money, I've only told you I've got something to sell, and given you first refusal. I'm not threatening anything."

"I told you—I couldn't raise anything like that sum."

"Make me an offer," Marguerite invited. "No, don't hurry, think it over. I'm sure you'll come to a reasonable conclusion. In the meantime, how about coming on the refugee committee?"

Hatty leaned back, her fingers interlaced. "All right," she said, after a moment. "Why not? You must tell me the date of the next meeting. After all, it's time I gave Burlham something new to talk about."

" Oh, yes, you're one of our prime subjects of conversation," Marguerite agreed. " Your marriage caught everyone short. Well, you can't be surprised, Philip Cobb was never in the running in the old days."

What she didn't say was as clear as what she did. An ambitious young man without much capital won't baulk at— well, damaged goods; not if there's a pleasant financial backing.

" You don't know my husband," repeated Hatty coolly. " He has a way of getting what he wants, what they call a bad enemy. Must you go now ? " She was on her feet and propelling her visitor towards the door. " Don't forget to let me know about the next meeting."

" Now, what's her game ? " thought Marguerite, unwontedly pensive as she turned to walk from Bridge Street up to the market place, where she would struggle for a place in the bus. It never occurred to her Hatty might not have one. In her experience life was like a game of Puss in the Corner. If you were Puss you were persistently on the alert to usurp someone else's corner, and once you'd got it you defended it tooth and claw. She'd got a corner now and she didn't intend to be elbowed out of it.

She had the natural vanity of the blackmailer ; it never occurred to her she might be in danger herself.

CHAPTER VII

HENRIETTA SAVAGE, driving through Brightling, was startled to see the figure of Marguerite Grey come round the corner of Bridge Street. She hadn't a doubt that she had been visiting Hatty, and she was equally sure that any visit from Marguerite spelt trouble. Quietly she drove alongside the small hurrying figure, and, letting down her car window, she called, " Miss Grey, are you going back to Burlham ? Can I give you a lift ? "

Marguerite's momentary anxiety changed instantly to a cool composure.

" How very kind ! I was just thinking I should have to wait for the bus. I've been calling on Hatty," she went on.

Since when have you called her Hatty ? Henrietta wondered. " Did she ask you ? " she inquired, drawing away from the kerb.

" Well, no, but it seemed to me so silly our cutting one another dead at every turn."

" I should hardly have thought you met often enough for that."

" I thought if she came on the refugee committee, then we should meet in quite unexceptional circumstances, and, anyway, that would be a beginning."

" I could have warned you you'd be wasting your time. Hatty was invited at the outset, but her house keeps her so busy."

" Oh, but I've made her change her mind," Marguerite assured her. " I think she was over-sensitive. She thought so long as it was you who asked her it might be regarded as —what's the word ?—nepotism. Now, no one could accuse me of trying to get a special friend in by the back door, could they ? "

Henrietta was so angry she almost drove into a stationary horse and cart.

"I'm sure you're glad," Marguerite went on. "It can't be good for her, moping about that little house all day. It must be a great change for her living in Bridge Street, after the parental mansion." She laughed prettily.

"It's usual for wives to live in the homes their husbands provide," Henrietta forced herself to say.

"Yes, and, of course, it's only a beginning. We all know Philip Cobb's bound to get on. They say in Brightling that poor Mr. Arbuthnot can't retire too soon for him. Cottage or churchyard, it's all one to the Cobbs."

"If you try and harm my daughter, Miss Grey, I'll make you sorry you were ever born," said Henrietta, as shocked as her companion to hear the words issue from her own lips, and at the same time she thought how easy it would be to overturn the car and dispose of both occupants. She saw Marguerite as a dose of deadly poison in a very pretty container.

"I harm Hatty? Why, Mrs. Savage, the boot's on the other foot. If it hadn't been for her—interference—I should be Mrs. Richard Sheridan by now, and as she's told everyone she didn't want him, you couldn't suggest I was stealing him from her. But I say let bygones be bygones; I'm getting established here, it's wonderful to me to have a firm background, and Hatty could help me. It's not asking a great deal, and after all, everyone wants to do something for the refugees. I'm helping with the costumes myself, I'm quite clever with my needle. I'm going to take part in one of the tableaux. I've got a wonderful black dress."

"What are you going to be? The Spirit of Compassion?"

"That wasn't kind. I'm going to be a refugee mother. I've got some Victorian dolls—Miss West's lending me one —if you could put me down at this corner I'll drop in and see if she'd let me have it now."

"How long have you known Hilda West?"

"Oh, we're great buddies. I'm trying to get her on to the committee, too. Old people shouldn't be allowed to retire into their shells."

"Why not, if they like their shells?"

"Because they become eccentric. Besides, we're all members one of another. I'm planning to draw her out."

"I suppose you appreciate you can't co-opt members on to the committee on your own account? You'll have to consult the others."

"Oh dear!" Marguerite shrugged prettily. "All this red tape. But if you'd suggest it, Mrs. Savage, there wouldn't be any argument at all. Everyone agrees with what you say."

More clearly than words her voice insisted, money talks.

"You can put it to them at their next meeting."

"If you insist. One does begin to wonder if all these formalities won't end by strangling Christian charity.

"I suppose it was Christian charity that sent you hot-foot round to my daughter this afternoon." Henrietta gave a snort that wouldn't have disgraced a good-sized pig. "You take care that Christian charity doesn't bring you to a sticky end."

When Philip Cobb got back that night he knew at once that something had happened. From his experience of other men's domestic felicities, a wife should leap up, crying, "Hallo, darling, is that you? I'll just take a peep in the oven while you set up the drinks." Or, alternatively, "For goodness' sake, come and open the bar. It's been the most ghastly day. The cleaner broke down and the milkman forgot to call."

This lovely stranger whom he had married simply said, "Hallo!" and waited for him to make the running.

"What sort of a day have you had?" He came over and stooped to kiss her; almost absently she turned her cheek.

"We're going to be on the map at last," said Hatty, composedly. "Marguerite Grey's been here."

Philip stiffened. "What did she want?"

"It's all right, darling. She only wants me to go on the refugee committee."

"But I thought you'd told your mother ..."

"You know how it is, the arguments of a contemporary are so much more persuasive. I said I'd attend the next meeting. I don't know what I can do, but don't they generally want a girl to make the tea and so on ? Or is that only in the Civil Service ? "

Beneath her brittle ease he saw that she was desperately unhappy. It was like being married to Siamese twins ; Hatty Savage and Mrs. Philip Cobb, they went about everywhere together, you couldn't get them apart. Sighing, he crossed to the cocktail cabinet someone had given them for a wedding present. Behind his back Hatty began to laugh.

" Husbands don't change much, do they ? In the Victorian age, when a man thought his wife was slightly hysterical, he recommended a nice glass of port. I don't know what they did in teetotal households, but perhaps wives there had too much sense to indulge in hysterics."

Philip mixed her a drink and put it into her hand.

" Look, darling," he said, " I know things haven't turned out quite the way we anticipated . . ."

" On the contrary," said Hatty composedly, " they've turned out exactly as I expected." She sipped her drink. " If ever you're hounded out of the legal world because of my reputation as one of the lucky ones that got away, you could do worse than run a bar. And I'm an expert in that field. I might even be able to give you a few tips."

He sat down on the arm of her chair, drawing her towards him.

" Hatty, why are you doing this ? "

" I told you, I've been invited. Mind you, I don't know what the rest of the committee will say. But I haven't had so many invitations since I came back that I can afford to disregard any of them."

" Well," said her husband, " it's not going to matter in future, because we shan't be here."

Her hand trembled, the glass tilted, a few drops fell on her knee. " Why not ? "

" I've got the chance of a practice up north. It wants a bit of pulling together, but it offers a good deal of scope, and I shall enjoy the challenge."

" Yes," she agreed, looking at the thin, intent face—was

it her imagination or had he really lost flesh during the past year ?—" I dare say you will, but what about me ? Suppose I don't want to be exiled ? This is my home town, and I'm not going to let a lot of gossips drive me out of it."

" Oh come, Hatty, that's unreasonable. You might have married a man sited in London . . ."

There was no thought of Alan Duke in his mind, but she winced.

" I didn't marry a man who lived in London, and you can wrap it up as nicely as you like, but it comes down to the same thing. We're being run out of town on a rail, because Richard Sheridan chose to commit suicide. Of course, it would be much more romantic and exciting if I had poisoned him, but I didn't, and I'm not going to give anyone a chance of saying I did. Can't you imagine ? " Her low voice, as savage as her name had been, mimicked one of Brightling's leading citizenesses. " They couldn't take it, my dear. Well, are you surprised ? Who wants a lawyer whose wife is probably a murderess ? Mind you, it was quite a scoop for young Cobb. John Savage is a very wealthy man . . ."

" Be quiet," her husband told her, but without violence. " You've brooded over this for so long you see nothing straight. I tell you, I want to take this practice, and between us we can put up the necessary money."

" Between us ? Oh, yes, the marriage settlement. What a strange idea to arrange it so that we can only draw on it by mutual consent."

" It's quite normal," Philip assured her. " If either party could draw without reference to the other, there'd be nothing to prevent an unscrupulous partner from drawing out the lot and disappearing into thin air. That sort of thing has happened too often for the legal profession not to be on its guard."

" So you can't buy the practice unless I agree ? "

" What have you got against it ? "

" I told you, it'll confirm everyone in the idea that I'm guilty and you know it, and we can't face the music."

" I don't know anything of the kind, any more than I

married you because your father's a rich man. Now, Hatty, this is really a great chance for us . . ."

But Hatty shook an obstinate head. "I shan't agree. I shall never agree. And if you could find the money yourself I still wouldn't let myself be driven out. Why, it would be worse than ever in a new place. Here at least we have friends."

"There no one would know our story."

"For how long? They'll start asking questions, the women anyhow, and pretty soon it'll be the mixture as before. Oh, yes, that new man, Cobb, isn't it? He was at Brightling, don't you remember, he married that girl who was said to have poisoned her lover, you know, a sort of modern Madeleine Smith—so lucky for her her father was a rich man . . ."

Philip said with a kind of quiet desperation, "What hopes are there for us so long as you keep up this attitude? Face the facts, there are no prospects for us here."

"Nonsense. Mr. Arbuthnot will retire in a year or two . . . ."

"He's had an offer from another quarter, cash down, and he's accepted it. He told me."

The painful colour stained her cheeks. "Did he tell you why? Never mind, it's obvious. It's because of me. But what an insult! After all the work you've done for him. Oh, it's not fair, just because I wrote some silly letters . . ."

"What's that?"

She realised she had gone too far. "It's nothing much," she said sullenly, like a child. "I wrote Richard some silly letters, there was nothing to them really . . ."

"Is that what Marguerite Grey knows? Is that why . . . ?"

"Richard seems to have told her a lot of nonsense—according to her, I mean."

"Is she blackmailing you?" He caught her shoulder in a furious grip. "Hatty, you've got to answer me."

Hatty pulled herself away. "If you call it blackmail asking me to come on her committee."

"Has she asked you for money?"

" Of course she hasn't. Where would I get money from ?
Besides, she wants something more than money. She wants
to wriggle in. She knows I can't refuse a perfectly reasonable
request. I shouldn't bring an action for slander whatever
she said."

" What could she say ? Hatty, I'm your husband, your
natural protector. What could she say ? "

" It depends on her imagination, I suppose."

" You never mentioned the letters before."

" I didn't think about them. Richard said he'd burnt
them, how was I to know what he'd told her ? "

" You mean, she has the letters ? "

" Yes," agreed Hatty.

" It wasn't true, what you told me, was it ? She is asking
for money ? "

" I haven't given her a penny," insisted Hatty.

" But—she has made demands ? "

" Now you know about the letters it doesn't matter, does
it ? "

" That would depend what was in them. Is there any
evidence . . . ? "

" Evidence of what ? That I killed him ? " She pulled
away and leapt to her feet. " You said you believed me."

" I do. How much harm would it do you if those letters
became public property ? "

" They were just love-letters. Well, if I'd been going to
poison him, do you suppose I'd have warned him ? "

" There were no threats ? "

" I don't know how I can be expected to remember
everything I wrote when I was in love. I expect they were a
bit extravagant. Love-letters generally are. We aren't all
lawyers, knowing how dangerous it is to commit ourselves.
. . . If I had to draw a picture of hell, do you know what it
would be ? An enormous mouth whispering into an
enormous ear. And never stopping. Because that's what
eternity means, doesn't it ? Something going on for ever
and ever."

" I'll have a word with Miss Grey . . ."

" No. You couldn't stop her."

" Stop her from doing what ? "

" She says she might take them to the papers."

" If she considers they throw any light on Richard's death, it's her duty to take them to the police."

" I've told you, they don't throw any light. But—I should die of shame if anyone else read them. Oh, Philip, I don't know what to do."

" Come north with me. I'll go ahead with the arrangements at once. If Miss Grey makes further trouble, refer her to me. And you needn't be afraid she'd try and follow us, she's far too comfortable here." He paused. " I wonder what her hold is over Miss Sheridan."

" Perhaps she has a dark secret, too. Perhaps Richard was really her son and there wasn't any brother killed by a bomb."

" It should be easy to prove or disprove that. The record would be at Somerset House. Anyway, after twenty years, would that kind of revelation do her much harm ? "

" You're forgetting the Nonconformist element, aren't you ? It's particularly strong in Brightling. A scarlet woman that's what they'd call her. The Clover House would suffer, and she couldn't bear that. She could bear for Richard to die, she could bear to see me ruined, but not her restaurant. When she dies, if they open her up to look for her heart, they'll find a little stone shaped like a hotel. . . ."

She wrung from him a promise that he would not approach Marguerite without telling her first ; but so far as the new practice was concerned he could make no headway with her. He was convinced there was no future for him in Brightling, and he had energy and ambition enough to resent playing second fiddle for the rest of his days. He confessed now that he had under-estimated the strength of local feeling against this marriage, now their best hope was to acknowledge the fact and make a fresh start. He was certain that so long as they remained in Brightling Hatty would refuse to bear him a child. He wrote to Smith, in the north, keeping the offer open ; but he was aware that in this at least Hatty was his worst enemy. No, she said, no and no and no. " I won't agree. It's all a question of patience. If

you can't be patient, then you can't really believe in me."
She flung up her arms. " Did you see the local paper this
week ? Aileen Butcher knocked down by a car and killed,
and she had a husband and three children. And John Hope
drowned last summer and Penny Payne dying when her
baby was born. It's happening all the time, good people,
useful people, with no sense at all, but never Marguerite
Grey. And yet, why shouldn't she die, Philip ? Why
shouldn't she die ? "

CHAPTER VIII

MARGUERITE AT THE breakfast table looked as dainty as her
name. Yellow dress, white bead necklace, the finest of sheer
nylons. She spread the butter about a quarter of an inch
thick on her toast.

" Aunt Alison," she said prettily, " I hope you don't
mind, I've invited the refugee sewing committee to meet
here. I really felt it was my turn."

Alison's face hardened. " It didn't occur to you to ask
me first ? "

Marguerite looked startled. " But what difference can it
make to you ? You'll be at the restaurant, and they'll be
gone before four at the latest."

" What time have you invited them ? "

" Actually, I said a fork luncheon. I'll do all the cooking."

" I'm sure you will," Alison agreed. " How about
expenses ? Do they come out of the fund ? You won't
make much profit at that rate, will you ? "

Marguerite, whose expressions could change in a manner
that would have delighted a stage director, now looked hurt.

" I didn't think you'd mind my charging them, they won't
be anything very big. They aren't expecting champagne and
oysters or anything like that. And you'd want to contribute
something to the refugees, wouldn't you ? "

" I might prefer to write a cheque direct."

" Well, you could do that, too, couldn't you ? Mrs. Savage and Hatty are coming."

" One of these days," prophesied Alison, with a kind of hard bitterness, " you'll batter your way into the Courts of Heaven through sheer insolence."

" I went to see Hatty. I thought it was silly to keep up a feud."

" You can't keep up a feud with someone you don't know," Alison pointed out.

" And, of course, she lives in rather a poky way now. I wanted to sort of draw her back."

" I couldn't have blamed her if she'd pushed you out of a window," Alison said in a more cheerful tone.

" I shouldn't think she'd want any more of that kind of publicity. Anyhow, I'm someone here and it's time everybody realised it."

" Just so long as you make sure you aren't someone in the churchyard," agreed Alison, in the same carefree way.

" What an extraordinary remark ! There seems to be a sort of epidemic going round. Because that makes three of you."

On the day of Marguerite's fork luncheon Henrietta arrived at Star Cottage fifteen minutes before she was due, and was surprised and rather put out to find Miss West on the doorstep. She had hoped for a few words alone with Marguerite, on whose shoulders she placed the responsibility for Hatty's present mood, which moved from alarming defiance to a kind of fury of despair. How long Philip could be expected to endure these domestic conditions she couldn't tell. Does he know Hatty is being threatened and, if so, by whom ? she wondered. She had tried to raise the question with her daughter, to be met with a point-blank refusal to say a word.

After her husband, Hatty was the dearest creature in the world to her, and Hatty, unlike John, needed her support. Little Miss Grey shall realise two can play at that game, she reflected grimly, marching to Star Cottage by the short cut. And now poor silly Miss West was going to ruin everything.

The old woman turned, with a tall, ageing dignity. " I'm

so glad you've come," she said. " I was afraid I'd mistaken the time. I thought the card said twelve-forty-five. Was that right ? "

" Isn't Miss Grey in ? " inquired Henrietta, not committing herself.

Miss West pointed to a neatly printed card in green ink that had been pinned beside the bell.

PLEASE WALK IN, it said.

" So extraordinary," murmured Miss West. " I rang but no one came, and I don't fancy the idea of finding myself alone on someone else's premises. Oh dear, I've forgotten my gloves." She seemed in a very agitated state.

" She must be in," said Henrietta, reassuringly. " Perhaps she's changing or something."

Miss West looked down her long aristocratic nose. Housemaids had changed when she was a girl, and parlour-maids, of course, but one's hostess . . . Still, Marguerite was more in the former category than the latter.

Henrietta pressed the bell, waited a moment, then said decidedly, " Let's go up. We can't stand about in this wind. Perhaps she's forgotten something and has run along to Stiles." (Stiles was the village shop, a kind of treasure trove where you could find practically anything.)

They went up to the first floor, where a door stood open. The table in the centre of the room was as polished as a looking-glass and was spread with dishes of mousse and trifle, a fish salad, every kind of sandwich, bridge rolls, sliced galantine on savoury toast and slabs of rich creamy cake. It would have given Crook what he called the collywobbles even to see it, but the refugee committee would be entranced.

Miss West, looking from dish to dish, said gently, " What an extraordinary meal. I suppose this is what is known as a spread." (People may be democrats in towns, but in the country they are expected to know their place.) Henrietta, more diplomatic, remarked enviously, " How does she get that sort of purple glow on the wood ? My girl will smear too much polish on and expect that to do all the work." Miss West said sedately, " When I was a child I was sent to the local shop for twopennyworth of elbow grease. I'll never forget how they laughed." Henrietta said, "There are some advantages to living in the Welfare State. Do you know, I don't believe I've been inside this house since Marguerite Grey came to share it."

They looked about them. It was a large room, divided by velvet curtains into a drawing-room and a dining-room. To-day the curtains were drawn. Presumably the goods collected for the sale were on show behind them, and in her own good time and with her usual sense of the dramatic, Marguerite would reveal them.

"I made hot-water bottle covers," breathed Miss West. "Old blanket with the moth in it, cut away the eaten parts and the rest is absolutely designed for such a use. I thought perhaps two and threepence, or would two shillings be better?"

Henrietta noticed with a sense of shock that the old woman was talking in a whisper. Worse, that she herself was inclined to drop her voice. She raised it to an artificial level.

"I'm a little surprised that Alison isn't here," she said. "Of course, the restaurant is important, but just for this occasion . . ."

"I dare say she had her instructions like the rest of us," retorted Miss West, in a high voice that suddenly rang through the room.

Henrietta turned and stared. "My dear Miss West, what can you mean? You're looking quite pale. Are you . . . ?"

"The heat," said Miss West. "And then, really, this young woman. The fact is, I have outlived my generation, I'm not in tune with the present age. Everything has changed. When I lived at home with my father—he was Canon of Nuncton, you know—I used to help a good deal with bazaars and whist drives. I was very good at whist. But we sold embroidered teacloths and tray mats, and we used to bring home-made jam and collect trinkets if we could persuade our friends to part with them, not these modern pictures—cubist, do they call them? I can't think how Miss Grey imagines she's going to sell that and these modern vases, all lop-sided . . ."

"Ceramics," contributed Henrietta, intelligently. "If Marguerite made all these," she added, walking round the laden dining-table, "she's wasting her time here. She'd be a gift to Alison at The Clover House."

"Oh, no," said Miss West quickly. "That would never do. Miss Sheridan would never let anyone take over any of her responsibility. But really one does wonder at her staying here . . ." She turned pink. "Not, of course, that it's any affair of mine."

"Oh, nonsense!" said Henrietta easily. "If there wasn't a bit of gossip how on earth should we get through the days? It's only taking an interest—I do wonder where Marguerite is. It seems very strange . . ."

Miss West was walking slowly round the room, her hands thrust into the pockets of her shabby ulster that was too warm for the day.

"Surely she doesn't think it matters not wearing gloves in the house," Henrietta reflected. She remembered hearing that her great-grandmother used to wear white gloves at breakfast. "It's very hot in here," she offered. "Perhaps Marguerite suffers from poor circulation. I wonder if one dare turn down that electric fire."

"Here is your daughter," remarked Miss West, who was standing at the window overlooking the street. "I think she's doing too much. She looks very pale. Of course, young women nowadays work so hard."

Hatty came in looking like a Valkyrie, her face warm from the wind. Where on earth did the old girl get the idea she was pale? Henrietta wondered. "Good heavens!" said Hatty. "Don't say Alison's giving all that food?"

"You didn't see any sign of Marguerite as you came, I suppose?" Henrietta murmured.

"Marguerite? Isn't she here?"

Henrietta looked round eloquently.

"Oh, well, perhaps she's dressing up. She's going to be part of a tableau on the day, you know. One thing, Lady Martin will be pleased. I suppose she's coming."

Lady Martin liked it to be known that she was county, though she looked more like a peasant than anyone else in the village. She wore aggressive tweeds and had an aggressive voice and believed in making it work.

" Here's Mrs. Waltham," murmured Hatty, and in she came, the widow of a man who'd made a packet in chain greengrocery stores, wearing a fur coat that wouldn't have disgraced a grizzly bear. She threw it off.

" Warm, isn't it ? " she said. " How about opening a window ? "

Lady Martin arrived as the clock struck the hour.

" Is Miss Sheridan not to be here ? " she demanded.

" We don't know," said Henrietta promptly. " Personally, I should be glad to see either of them."

The last two members of the committee arrived five minutes later, two youngish married women, called Dangerfield and Dacre—they called each other David and Jonathan.

" Better late than never," said David gaily.

Lady Martin fixed her with a glaucous green eye. " You should have that made into a gramophone record," she observed.

Mrs. Dacre laughed, a little unconvincingly. " My mother wanted me to be a Valentine," she confided. " But I was six hours late, born at daybreak on February the fifteenth. I've been chasing those six hours all my life."

Lady Martin muttered something that sounded like " Plenty of practice," and then Mrs. Dangerfield said brightly, " At least we don't seem to be the last. Where's Marguerite Grey ? "

" Having a bath," giggled Mrs. Dacre. She went on tiptoe to the door, putting a would-be roguish finger to her lip. " Not a sound," she hissed.

" Perhaps she's gone to buy flowers," hazarded Mrs. Waltham.

" Perhaps she's fainted," suggested Henrietta suddenly.

" Lying prone behind the curtain," agreed Mrs. Dangerfield breezily. With a sweeping gesture she rattled back the curtains on their wooden rings. " Good heavens, look at that picture. Tom Jordan took it for a bad debt years and years ago, and it's been up in the attic. Oh ! " Her voice changed to a kind of suppressed shriek. Because there she was, Marguerite Grey, the missing hostess. She'd been there all the time while they talked about her, drooped picturesquely above a little desk, her head sunk on her hands ; she was wearing an extraordinary black dress that came almost to her feet, with a handsome fine black cashmere shawl draped crookedly over her shoulders.

" Oh, look ! " said Enid Dacre, who was what Mrs. Waltham called no more than ninepence in the shilling. " She's got some little dolls—I suppose they're meant to be refugee children. They're rather sweet, aren't they ? "

" Don't ! " cried Mrs. Waltham.

And screamed.

From her position by the window old Miss West stiffened ; Hatty turned briskly.

" What on earth . . . ? Oh ! "

Lady Martin took two quick steps forward and came to a dead stop. Only Henrietta went close to the motionless, the frozen figure. Under the maladjusted shawl they could all now perceive the handle of the long delicate knife thrust between the dead girl's shoulders.

Mrs. Dacre opened her mouth. " Don't panic ! " commanded Henrietta. " We must telephone for a doctor."

" Telephone for the police," corrected Lady Martin. " And tell them to send an ambulance. No doctor's going to help us here."

" How can you be sure ? " whispered a white-faced Mrs. Dangerfield.

" How would you feel with a knife in your back ? " demanded Lady Martin brutally.

Old Miss West turned reluctantly from the window. " I believe I have heard of conjurers' knives that have a collapsible blade," she offered nervously.

" Very clever," snorted Lady Martin, who never minded what she said or to whom she said it. " Perhaps you can explain how anyone, short of a snake, could manage to put a knife between her own shoulders."

" Poor Miss Sheridan ! " whispered Mrs. Waltham. " What a dreadful thing to happen in your house."

"Dreadful thing to happen anywhere," retorted Lady Martin.

"You mean, it's murder?" quavered Enid Dacre.

"Of course not, it's a game of Scrabble." Lady Martin believed that if you were rich enough you could be as rude as you pleased. "Hatty, what's the matter with you? Can't you use the telephone?"

"She's had a shock," said Henrietta quickly. "I'll ring. Where is it?"

"In the hall," said old Miss West. "Such a public place to keep a telephone."

Henrietta went away; Hatty half hesitated, then stayed where she was. They all sent furtive, hurriedly removed glances at the dead girl. In her strange dress, her face half hidden, she didn't seem the Marguerite Grey they all knew. The dress might have belonged to some Victorian house-keeper, a tight-fitting bodice fastening down the back with a series of minute hooks and eyes, a flowing skirt stitched to a petersham band. It takes you right back, thought Mrs. Waltham, whose grandmother had actually been a house-keeper.

Henrietta came back. "They're sending a man at once, that Inspector Ferrers, I dare say. And I left a message for Alison. She was in the dining-room, so I asked if she could come back at once, there had been an accident."

She spoke mechanically; she was thinking, "Thank God, this is something they can't try and fasten on to Hatty. Because I was here before she was, and Hilda West can bear me out." An instant later she was horrified to realise the direction of her thoughts. Eighteen months before such an idea would never, never have entered her mind. In those days you couldn't imagine anyone thinking of Hatty as a potential murderess. Because, though they were all so different and their thoughts ran in as many diverse ways as ants rushing from their heap, there was no doubt in any mind that this was murder.

Hatty spoke at last. "Who killed her?" she asked.

Mrs. Dacre burst into an extraordinary sound, something between a boohoo and a giggle.

" I was thinking," she explained, " Miss Sheridan will never be able to use that knife again."

" If you don't control yourself," warned Lady Martin coldly, " I shall slap your face. I never heard such behaviour in the presence of death."

That sobered her at once. They all stood about, avoiding each other's eyes, until Mrs. Dangerfield said, " My husband and I were taking friends to dine at The Clover House to-night. I wonder if one should ring up."

No one had any comment to make there. Miss West said in a high, old voice, " Curiosity killed the cat. I always warned her she was too inquisitive for her own good."

Mrs. Waltham said, " I suppose we shall be in the Sunday papers now."

Hatty said, " I wonder if we could send the food to a hospital. It seems such a waste."

Lady Martin said, " They tell you you shouldn't touch anything," staring round defiantly as though someone was likely to snatch a sandwich or a bridge roll.

Henrietta said, " The police are taking a very long time." It was like some dreadful nightmare card game, everyone playing from his hand and nobody bothering to follow suit.

As Henrietta had prophesied, Ferrers was in charge of the case. Lady Martin, assuming instant control, told him nothing had been touched, and looked meaningly at the table. Ferrers asked who had found the body and Mrs. Waltham said with a sort of hiccup that in a way she had, as she didn't think anyone else had realised it was a body, if the inspector knew what she meant, not till she screamed.

Ferrers said he'd want a statement from each of them, and turned instinctively to Henrietta, who explained why they were there. She added, " I came a little early—I wanted a word with Miss Grey in connection with committee matters "—she told the untruth quite calmly—" and I found Miss West had just arrived. We came up together."

Miss West said quickly, " I mistook the time, I thought Miss Grey had said twelve-forty-five."

Lady Martin said, " No one warned me it was a fancy

dress affair." Hatty thought, " She looks just like her pug, Prinny. They say animals and people grow to resemble each other." And it was common knowledge that Prinny got a lot softer treatment than Sir Reginald.

" I know Miss Grey wanted a tableau at the fête," said Henrietta, still composed, thinking, " God's wonderful. Nothing between us and our terrors but a frontal of skin and bone, and no one can see them, no one." Though, if anyone could, it would be this quiet gimlet-eyed man to whom murder seemed just another name in the book.

Enid Dacre gave another of her fatuous giggles. " Dress rehearsal," she said. " Are you sure she's really dead ? "

" The doctor's on his way," said the inspector, but he hadn't any doubts, and he knew they hadn't either.

He asked about Alison and learned that she had been sent for. Miss West said unexpectedly that one of the dolls the dead girl was supposed to be caressing was hers, she had lent it under duress, would be glad to be allowed to take it back.

" Practically an heirloom," she explained.

" All in good time," said Ferrers.

" Can't think how you came to lend her anything valuable for this kind of folderol," snapped Lady Martin. " Everyone knows that things lent for a bazaar never come home to roost."

Ferrers thought, " She's got something there. What's the old girl doing in this bunch anyway ? "

But he knew he'd find out in due course.

" Miss Grey is very persuasive, was very persuasive," amended Miss West defensively. " And such a good cause. She wanted to enlist everyone's help, and really practically no one had been able to resist her."

That was a dig at Lady Martin, who hadn't been able to keep her fat paws off even a committee more or less dominated by an outsider.

" Indeed ? " sniffed Lady Martin. " Making a show of other people's misery, I call it. But that was the young woman all over. A born exhibitionist. Look at the way she bounced up at young Sheridan's inquest. Any decent body would have made a statement to the police in the normal way."

"It's the shock," said Mrs. Dangerfield complacently, and you realised how she was going to capitalise that in the days ahead. "My dear, I was actually there when the body was found." "Oh, well," thought Ferrers, "vultures are the same all the world over, no matter what shape they assume."

Then the doctor arrived and confirmed that Marguerite was dead, though, like most of his profession, he was cagey when it came to setting a precise time. Electric fires were burning in both rooms, the body was muffled in this heavy black dress, with its shawl atop.

"Who saw her alive last?" he demanded, "apart from the murderer, of course."

No one present would admit to having seen her that day at all.

"She was alive at twelve o'clock," said Hatty unexpectedly. "She rang me up." And as she spoke she recalled the soft voice saying in a confidential whisper, "You know who this is. I'll expect you at twelve-thirty. Don't forget what I told you." And then silence coming down again like a theatre curtain.

Henrietta barely repressed a start. "What did she say?" she exclaimed.

Ferrers gave her a reproachful glance. "Just asked me if I could come a bit early to help with arrangements," said Hatty.

"And you did?"

"No. That is, I set out, but my car conked out in Beggar's Alley. That's the short cut in from Brightling. It took me twenty minutes to get her going again. There wasn't a soul about. You know what the place is like on a Wednesday. Marketeers go into Brightling to do their shopping."

"You called the garage, perhaps?" Ferrers murmured, but Hatty said, "Of course not. I can do simple repairs myself. My father only gave me a car on the understanding that I'd learn to cope with minor emergencies."

John Savage's reputation was well enough known for no one to query that. No one, he held, should be in charge of a machine whose workings remained a mystery to him. Clever with his hands himself, he had little sympathy for fools who rang up a mechanic to put in a screw.

"My daughter didn't arrive till after Miss West and myself," said Henrietta.

Hilda West surprised them by saying, "Miss Grey telephoned me, too. I didn't notice the time particularly but it was probably about twelve o'clock."

"Any special reason, Miss West?"

"Just to remind me I was expected."

"Did she think you might forget?"

"I think perhaps she thought I might forget on purpose. It's so long since I played any part in social life . . ." Her voice trailed painfully away. Everybody knew her weakness, she was quite aware of that, though nobody would admit it publicly.

"Did she telephone anyone else?" Ferrers looked expectantly at the gathering, but he got no response. Their eyes were like curtained windows. The girl might have been a danger to them living, but she could be just as dangerous to them dead.

"I have thought of something," declared Lady Martin. "There is, I understand, a back door to this house, a gate opening on to a lane. The front door was standing open when I arrived, there was nothing to prevent the murderer hiding upstairs and stealing down while we waited for you." She glared at Ferrers. "The stairs are carpeted, I noticed that, no one has left this room, except Mrs. Savage to telephone . . ."

Mrs. Dacre screamed, "He might be here still."

"How long was the front door open?" Ferrers asked, as the constable unobtrusively left the room.

But no one could tell him. Miss West said she found it on the jar when she arrived about 12.45.

"The card was in place. I think Miss Grey must have written that, she always affected this ridiculous green ink. at least, the two post cards I ever had from her were written in green."

The dead girl's bag was set at her feet under the shadow

of that overwhelming black dress. When it was examined a cheap ball-point pen was found, loaded with green.

The doctor said it was quite probable Marguerite had never known what hit her; she might have lived a short time after the blow was struck, but it would only be a matter of minutes in his opinion, and she would lose consciousness at once.

Ferrers indicated a large gilt-edged looking-glass hanging on the wall.

" Why didn't she see her assailant in that ? " he wondered. " But, of course, she probably did. Wouldn't be the first time a lamb had been deceived by a wolf in sheep's clothing." He looked back at the women who had insensibly drawn closer together, as though they stood on opposite sides of a moat. " Seven of them," he reflected, " and not a word of compassion between them."

" That only means they ain't hypocrites," said the doctor, reading his thoughts. " Wouldn't surprise me if more than one of them sleeps better to-night knowing Marguerite Grey will be in the mortuary. No, I'm not giving evidence, but I'm a doctor and we get around. She was like one of those pretty little flowers, sun-dews, aren't they, that lure insects by their nice bright colouring, and then suddenly close up over them, and that's the end. I've always wondered why Miss Sheridan agreed to have her here, but it wouldn't surprise me to know there was something queer about that boy and she'd learned it. Miss Sheridan thought the world of Richard."

Long years of practice had enabled him to talk out of the corner of his mouth so that no one but the person he was addressing could hear what he said. " Wonder what Mrs. Cobb is doing here ? " he went on. " In the circumstances, you'd expect the pair to be at daggers drawn."

He gave the inspector a wry grin. " Daggers is about it," he said. Then he turned away and looked at the laden table.

" Lot of muck," he remarked in his outspoken way. " Why can't people eat honest food ? Oh, well, must remember the patent medicines boys, they have to get their living like the rest of us."

" Do you need us here any longer ? " demanded Mrs. Dangerfield. " Mrs. Dacre and I didn't arrive till after one o'clock, and everyone else was here by then. And we came straight from Brightling, so being unpunctual has its virtues too." She glared defiantly at Lady Martin.

Lady Martin remembered suddenly, " I telephoned at twelve-thirty. Always confirm appointments, people are so forgetful."

" Did Miss Grey answer the phone ? "

" No one answered."

" But you came just the same ? "

" Rang Mrs. Savage. I knew she'd be there if the thing hadn't been put off."

" Yes," agreed Henrietta. " I was just leaving the house."

" Twelve-thirty, you said ? "

" I told you, Inspector, I intended to be a little early."

" No one else rang Miss Grey ? "

No one else had.

Ferrers told them they could go, but he'd want their individual statements in due course.

" No one touched the knife, I suppose ? " he added.

" Well, of course not," replied Enid Dacre. " We're not ghouls."

" I may have to ask you for your finger-prints," Ferrers warned them.

" You'll find those all right," prophesied Mrs. Dangerfield scornfully. " We've all touched something while we were waiting."

" He means the knife," said Mrs. Waltham in a jerky voice.

" Does anyone recognise it ? " Ferrers asked.

" It's one of Miss Sheridan's," agreed Henrietta. " I suppose it was on the table, and someone snatched it up . . ."

The inspector saw them off the premises. Unless Henrietta and old Miss West were conniving with one another, they were all in the clear, he thought. Seven people in one plot was too much for even him to swallow. Besides, you want a motive, and the person with a possible motive was Hatty Cobb, and there had been two other people present when she arrived.

The sergeant had gone through the upper part of the house by the time the party had taken itself off, but there was no sign of any intruder, no one under the bed, nothing disturbed. No tell-tale cigarette end or even a little dribble of ash, no one in the wardrobe, no evidence of someone escaping from a bathroom window. The finger-print squad would do their stuff next and they might find something helpful on a door handle, except, he commented morosely, those whodunnit chaps have blown the gaff so often that nowadays if you did find finger-prints on the scene of a crime you could bet your bottom dollar they didn't belong to the criminal. As if police work wasn't tricky enough, with staff shortages and insufficient pay, even the television had lined itself up with the wrong side. And he reminded Ferrers, who didn't require reminding, of a recent police court case where a young chap had followed the directions of an ex-con. in some magazine, and stolen a car, with no previous experience at all.

Alison arrived while they were still searching. She said she had left the house, as usual on a Wednesday, at about 11.30, at which time Marguerite seemed absorbed in preparations for the luncheon.

" It was quite a milestone for her," Alison told them. " She hadn't been hostess at anything like that since I knew her, probably never. She'd taken a great deal of trouble. Mind you," she added, " I'd no notion she was going to dress up for the occasion. She'd been altering the dress for some days . . ." Suddenly her tone changed. " That's my mother's shawl she's wearing," she exclaimed. " Where did she get that from ? "

It was a beautiful thing, very soft merino, in mint condition, with a soft fleecy fringe.

" You didn't keep it locked up, Miss Sheridan ? "

" No, of course not. It was in one of my drawers, but she hadn't asked if she might use it. Oh, well," she shrugged,

" I suppose she thought no one could refuse her anything for her precious refugees. I purposely didn't speak of it because I really rather treasure it. What really annoys me," she added, " is her leaving my house open to any Tom, Dick and Harry, without a word to me."

" Do you identify the writing on the card as hers ? " Ferrers inquired.

" Oh, yes. She makes that extraordinary ' E.' It's as good as a signature. Of course, she meant to wait till every-one had arrived, and then, I suppose, pull back the curtain and create a sensation. And that, at least," she added grimly, " she has certainly done."

She seemed to see the crowded table for the first time. " How many people was she expecting ? " she exclaimed. " There's enough for a dozen there."

You could see the thought moving through her mind like a goldfish in a tank, Sergeant Bartlett told his wife that evening, " wondering if she could take the stuff along to her restaurant in Brightling. You never saw any-thing like it, Maisie. Why, for the work she'd done on that she could have turned you out a steak-and-kidney pudd. and an apple pie, something worth putting in your insides."

But Mrs. Bartlett, who was suspected of Commie sym-pathies, said darkly that was the gentry all over, kickshaws all the time, and nourishing food only fit for the working classes.

It was in the kitchen that the police made their momentous discovery. The light that began to glimmer there had soon shot up into a bonfire. Because in the kitchen stove, that was only intended to burn anthracite, they found a great wodge of newly-incinerated papers, packed down and ground more or less to ash.

When Alison saw that she really let fly. " What on earth has Marguerite been doing ? " she exclaimed, as though Marguerite wasn't stiff and stark next door, and for the moment Sergeant Bartlett thought, she probably had for-gotten. " She knows we mustn't burn rubbish here. There's an incinerator in the garden. What is it anyway ? " she

added, poking her head forward like a tortoise coming out of
its shell.

" Doing a bit of spring cleaning perhaps," suggested
Bartlett, woodenly.

" We're not living in the Middle Ages," snapped Alison.
" All that turning a house upside down once a year is a thing
of the past. We stay clean all the year round now, not just
once in the twelve months."

Bartlett looked injured, as though he thought the comment
a criticism of Mrs. B.'s capacities.

" It's enough to choke the dampers," Alison went on.
" What on earth was she getting rid of, anyway ? "

" We'll be able to tell you soon," Ferrers promised.

" How on earth can you tell with that mess ? " Alison
inquired.

" Spring cleaning isn't the only thing that's come up to
date," Ferrers told her. " Plenty of people don't realise
that burnt papers can be reconstituted and their original
nature identified. I'd say these were mostly letters," he
added. " Would you know anyone who wrote to Miss Grey
at this length ? "

" I don't really know very much about Miss Grey's
affairs. She may have had them a long time." But she wore
a puzzled look.

The powers that be were on the side of the police, for
once, for when they had raked out most of the ash, assembling
it carefully on a tin tray, Ferrers found, at the back of the
stove, a scrap of paper that had been blown back by the
draught and that, though scorched and brittle, could be
identified. It contained only a few words of no particular
significance, but the hand-writing was small and firm and
inscribed in a very black ink.

" That's not Miss Grey's writing," said Ferrers, and that
was a statement.

" Of course not," agreed Alison. " Nor is it mine," she
added dryly.

" Do you recognise it ? "

" Yes. But—it makes no sense, Inspector. Why on earth
should Hatty Cobb be writing to Miss Grey ? "

But Ferrers said in his dry fashion that until some of the papers had been reconstituted there was no proof that the letters had been written to Miss Grey.

It was not difficult to establish the fact that the letters had been written to the late Richard Sheridan.

Alison frowned. "But how did they come into Marguerite's possession?" she demanded. "He would never have given them to her."

"Then perhaps she found them somewhere," suggested Ferrers. "She never spoke of them to you?"

"Never. Why destroy them now, though? It would make more sense if she had given them back to the girl who wrote them. Didn't you say that Marguerite had rung up Mrs. Cobb and asked her to come early?"

"Mrs. Cobb says so."

"Perhaps she was going to give them back, and then, when Hatty didn't come . . ." She met the inspector's impassive green gaze.

"Mrs. Savage and Miss West were here at twelve-forty-five," he reminded her. "Besides, with all that paper being burned you'd expect to find ash on the hands."

"No one else could have burned them," Alison insisted. "They weren't in the stove when I left the house—at least . . ." She stopped. "Oh, no, she'd never have the nerve to burn them while I was about. I suppose she thought she could clear the stove before I got back."

"It's not surprising if Mrs. Cobb was dancing to Miss Grey's pipes," Ferrers observed a bit later. "These letters are dynamite. Might throw a bit of fresh light on young Sheridan's death. I was never satisfied about the verdict there. And if you can tell me why that girl should burn a virtual gold-mine . . ."

Bartlett opened his big countryman's eyes. "Thinking perhaps she didn't burn them?"

"I'm wondering if a considerable sum's been paid into Miss Grey's account lately. Shouldn't be hard to find that out."

It wasn't. Nothing had been paid into Marguerite's account during the previous week.

" Then the money should be in the house," insisted Ferrers. But there was no sign of that.

Then a local jeweller came forward with the information that Marguerite had asked him to set aside a pair of diamond ear-rings, saying she was expecting a considerable remittance during the next few days and asking if he would hold them for a week. Alison said, " I've no notion where she expected to get the money, certainly not from me."

Ferrers could make a pretty good guess. But, like Monty, he believed that the man who wins his battles is the man who has reserves of ammunition. He started making inquiries in a number of directions and came up with some unexpected information before he decided to make his call on Mrs. Philip Cobb.

CHAPTER IX

WHEN RICHARD SHERIDAN died in mysterious circumstances fifteen months before, John Savage had warned his daughter, " Don't make any statements without getting legal advice." Now her husband was saying practically the same thing.

" Why did Miss Grey telephone you in the first place and ask you to come earlier than the others ? " he insisted.

" I suppose she wanted to talk to me."

" You know she wanted to talk to you. Was it about the letters ? "

" How do I know ? I didn't see her."

" Oh, don't be so stupid, Hatty. Of course you knew what she wanted to see you about. Use a little of your natural intelligence. The police are going to ask you all these questions. You want to be prepared."

" Since I didn't see her how can I be sure what she wanted ? I can't tell the police more than that. I know she's dead, I know it was murder. Everyone in the neighbourhood knows that. And that's all I can say."

" Can you prove you didn't get there at half past twelve ? "

Hatty stared. " Well, of course. Mother and old Miss West were there when I arrived."

" Oh yes. But can you prove where you were at, say, twelve-thirty ? Don't say you were at home, because I rang you up at twelve-fifteen and there was no reply."

" Of course there wasn't any reply. I was bogged down in Beggar's Alley."

" Did anyone see you there ? Do think, Hatty. After all, the whole of Burlham wasn't in Brightling."

" Too bad none of them happened to be in the alley."

" Did you speak of the breakdown to anyone before the girl's body was found ? "

" I never had the chance."

" You might have said something to the committee while you were waiting for Miss Grey to appear."

" Well, I didn't. Mother would only have asked why I was going there early, and if you knew how sick you get of being asked questions . . ."

" You're going to get a lot sicker before we're through," her husband warned her grimly. " You see, Ferrers may take the view that there was no breakdown, that you kept your twelve-thirty appointment, went out by the side door, and came back about twelve-fifty or whatever it was to establish your alibi."

" I thought even police had to prove their theories."

" Has it occurred to you they'll find your letters ? "

" It might be quite a good thing if they did. If I'd murdered her, I'd have removed them, wouldn't I ? " Impatiently she lighted a cigarette and threw the match on the carpet. " Why do lawyers always have to look on the black side of things ? " she demanded. " I wasn't there, so no one can prove I was. Of course, if I'd known she was going to get herself knifed I'd have provided myself with an alibi."

" Had she any hold over you beside the letters ? "

" Don't you think they're enough ? Tell me, suppose I admitted to you that I did know more than I've said, what

would your reaction be ? No, I really want to know. Would
you throw me to the wolves in the sacred name of Ter-
ewth ? ''

" There are times," said Philip in a low, choked voice,
" when I could willingly strangle you myself."

The knife fell the next day when Ferrers came to the
house and asked Hatty if she could identify the scrap of
paper they had taken from the stove.

" What do you expect me to say about it ? " Hatty
demanded. " It's my hand-writing—that's all I can tell
you."

" Whom was it written to ? "

" Why, Marguerite, I suppose. Unless it was to Miss
Sheridan. There are only about four words . . ."

" It's only a specimen," Ferrers told her quietly.

He saw her hands catch and cling. " We've been able
to reconstitute a good many of the other papers," he
added.

" What other papers ? "

" The ones we found in the stove at the cottage."

" You didn't say there were any others."

" You didn't know ? "

" Of course I didn't know. Oh well, I suppose Miss
Sheridan had been turning out her desk."

" According to Miss Sheridan, she never burned papers
in her stove."

" Then I suppose it was Marguerite."

" Did you often write to Miss Grey, Mrs. Cobb ? Can
you remember, for instance, when you last wrote to her ? "

" I don't remember ever writing to her," acknowledged
Hatty carelessly. She was the child of her generation. Why
put pen to paper for run-of-the-mill matters if there was a
telephone handy ?

" In any case, these letters weren't written to Miss
Sheridan. The contents would tell us that. Have you
any of the writing-paper you normally use handy, Mrs.
Cobb ? "

She pulled open a drawer and showed him a box. " Not

that any stationer will ever make a fortune off me," she said.

Ferrers took the sheet she offered. " This isn't the same kind of notepaper."

" Why should it be ? This is the paper my husband buys."

" Which seems to show that the letters were written before your marriage. Mrs. Cobb, at one time you wrote letters to the late Richard Sheridan."

" Oh, yes, but that was ages ago. And he burnt them."

Philip, who was present as her legal adviser, shook his head. Women were extraordinary, they hung on to hope when there was no hope left. It was absurd now to try and disguise the nature of Ferrers's find.

" Mrs. Cobb, there's no sense in all this fencing. We can prove that these letters were written by you to Richard Sheridan and were presumably in Miss Grey's possession. Had she spoken of them to you ? "

" What are you asking me to do ? Condemn myself out of my own mouth ? "

Ferrers was in no way disconcerted. " Mrs. Cobb, we've been making inquiries into your movements previous to Miss Grey's death. It appears you were out all day on Tuesday."

" I didn't know I had to get a police permit to take my own car out. It's licensed and insured . . ."

" You stopped for petrol at the Redcliffe Garage."

" Very likely."

" You took in six gallons."

" Did I ? It's quite likely. I generally fill the tank up. I never see the point in buying petrol in small quantities."

She was talking too much and too fast. Her husband leaned against the wall, his hands dug into his coat pockets. Ferrers went on like a machine, no emphasis, no haste.

" And you bought another supply of petrol on Thursday."

" Did I ? I don't keep accounts, you know, and anyway I book the petrol."

" Exactly."

" Oh, I see. You checked up with the Redcliffe. All right. So I bought some more on Thursday."

" And on Wednesday you only used the car to come to Miss Sheridan's house. So you must have gone about a hundred and fifty miles on Tuesday."

" Why not ? " asked Hatty insolently.

" You don't have to answer, of course, not at this stage, but would you care to tell me where you went ? "

" Why not ? I went to the coast."

" Alone ? "

" Certainly."

" To see a friend perhaps ? "

" No."

" Just for the spin ? "

" Just for the spin."

" I think I should tell you, Mrs. Cobb, that we know you stopped at Whiteside. The number of your car was noted by a constable for being wrongly parked."

She showed her first signs of panic. " He said there would be no charge. I didn't know . . ."

" There's no charge, but he made a note of the number."

" Well, if there's no charge . . ."

" The car was parked outside a jeweller's called Jevons."

" Very likely."

" We've seen Mr. Jevons. He has identified a photograph as being that of a woman who sold him some jewellery that afternoon."

" There isn't any law that prevents me selling my own jewellery, is there ? Oh dear, policemen seem to be like cats, they must do everything the longest way round. Why didn't you ask me straight away if I'd been selling jewellery ? Or were you afraid I'd deny it ? I'm not that stupid. I expect he showed you the things."

Ferrers put his hand in his pocket and brought out a small white box. Inside were a ring, a pendant and a brooch.

" Do you identify these as the articles you sold to Mr. Jevons for three hundred pounds ? "

Hatty nodded.

" Would you care to tell me why you sold them ? "

" I should have thought it was obvious. I wanted some spending money. My husband will warn you I'm very extravagant. Badly brought up," she added in a flippant voice, taking another cigarette.

Philip took his hands out of his pockets to hold a lighter to the tip ; he noticed it wasn't quite steady.

" Did you need the money to give to Miss Grey ? "

" Oh dear! " said Hatty with mock contrition. " I ought to have consulted you, oughtn't I, darling, then you could have given me the right answers. Miss Grey was trying to raise money for her refugees. That's right. *Her* refugees. You'd have thought she had a corner in them."

" If it was for that purpose, why not give the jewellery as it stood ? "

" It might have caused comment if she'd appeared wearing my jewellery. Oh, what's the use of all this hypocrisy ? Of course it wasn't for the refugees. She wanted it for herself."

" And she offered you the letters in exchange ? "

" Yes, I suppose so."

" How much did she ask for ? "

" A thousand pounds." Philip's breath drew in on the faintest of whistles. " Well, of course I had no intention of giving her anything like that, and I don't suppose she ever thought I would."

" Did you offer her the three hundred ? "

" I didn't get the chance. She was dead when I arrived."

" Yes. Of course. Have you the money still ? "

" I have. I can show it you. Won't that prove I didn't see her ? " A wild hope lit up her voice.

" I'm afraid it would only prove you didn't give her the three hundred pounds."

" I'm not such a fool that I can't see what you're getting at," cried Hatty recklessly, " but you're wrong. I didn't get to the house before about ten minutes to one, and my mother and Miss West will tell you the same. Why, I don't for a minute suppose I'm the only person Marguerite Grey was trying to blackmail. How do you suppose she persuaded all the others to come to heel the way they did ? Look at old Miss West, she hasn't been out for I don't know how long, but Marguerite only had to ring her up and along she came." She caught sight of her husband's horrified face. " I'm not suggesting she's concerned in this," she added quickly. " Poor old thing, it's probably as much as she can do to cut the top off an egg, but Marguerite was ambitious, and she couldn't hope to make herself independent on what I could afford to give her. And anyway, if I had seen her and got the letters, do you suppose I'd be fool enough to leave them on the premises ? "

" They were in the kitchen stove. It might be thought safer to put them there than to chance being found with them in your possession."

" Here we go round the mulberry bush, the mulberry bush, the mulberry bush," chanted Hatty. " You think I killed her, I know I didn't. Where do we go from here ? "

Philip knew the answer to that, if she didn't. Inwardly he seethed with fury, less against the police who were only doing their job, than against his silly, stubborn wife who was making the very worst of a bad case. It might seem illogical that his main desire at that moment was for a hand-grenade or something equally deadly to pulverise this pitiless investigator into a puff of dust. He spelt danger with a capital D to them both.

" I wonder if you aren't making too much of the letters, Inspector," he said, speaking for the first time for quite a while. " Suppose Miss Grey had sent them to me in fulfilment of her threat, well, I knew they existed, my wife had told me . . ."

" When was this, sir ? " Ferrers's voice was full of suspicion.

" I don't recall the exact date but it was before she died, oh, three or four weeks ago, I think."

" You knew she was threatening your wife ? "

" I didn't know she'd descended to blackmail, but I thought she was employing them as a weapon to engage my wife "—he hesitated—" I hardly like to say in her defence, but she was very anxious to establish herself in Burlham, and naturally Mrs. Cobb having lived here all her life would be a valuable ally."

" I see." Ferrers sounded about as sympathetic as a wooden figure-head, which at that moment he greatly resembled. " But is there any evidence that Miss Grey intended to send you the letters ? "

" Well, who else ? "

" She might have threatened to send them to Mr. Savage."

" He wouldn't have read them," said Hatty scornfully.

" There is a market for this kind of thing in the less reputable Press," Ferrers persisted. " And the Sheridan case was never finally closed, it could be re-opened at any time."

" What are you saying ? " Philip demanded.

" I think the court verdict might have been more definite if these letters had been read to them."

" I thought they were burnt," said Hatty, white to the lips.

" Some of them have proved decipherable. Was that the nature of her threat, Mrs. Cobb ? "

" Don't answer that, Hatty," said Philip in sharp tones. " It's true that Miss Grey was trying to make trouble, but her sole idea was to get money out of my wife."

" Had you advised her to pay ? "

" I wasn't aware she had asked for money—I told you that a minute ago—if I had been I should certainly have counselled a flat refusal and a threat of legal proceedings. I'm sorry my wife didn't confide in me completely, as I might have been able to save her a great deal of wretchedness. Miss Gray played on my wife's feelings for me, assuming she could wreck my professional reputation perhaps, or at all events smudge it."

" And, of course, sir, she could do nothing of the kind ? "

" Of course not. Confidentially, Inspector, I'm in treaty for a practice in the north—a fact of which I can offer you tangible proof—and I hardly think Miss Grey would have sacrificed a remarkably comfortable billet here to try and make difficulties for us once we were gone. Now, is there anything more you would like to ask me? I don't think my wife has anything else to tell you."

Ferrers got up. "That'll do for the moment, Mr. Cobb," he said. "You'll be seeing us again, no doubt. I take it you're not thinking of going away for a few days."

"Like yourself, I'm a working man," Philip assured him. "No, you'll find us here when you want us, though, as I say, I don't think there's anything more we can tell you."

"We haven't told him anything yet," said Hatty scornfully. "He's been telling us and most of the time he's been telling us wrong."

Philip went to see his visitors off the premises. When he came back he looked even graver than his wont.

"Do you remember the Oscar Wilde trial?" he asked. "Wilde was so sure of himself, so eager to score off his traducers he threw his hand away when he told the court that one of the young men named was a particularly ugly boy. That was the turning-point in his career."

"And what have I said that was so dangerous?"

"You were too obviously on the defensive."

"Anybody would be on the defensive with the police trying to accuse them of a murder they hadn't committed."

"Sit down and relax," her husband advised her. "Hatty, what was in those letters that made them so dangerous?"

"I told you, they were love-letters. If you'd ever written any you'd know the sort of thing."

"I don't think it's the love-letters they're interested in. After all, you never made any secret of the fact that at one time you were very *éprise* with young Sheridan. What else did you write to him?"

"Well, I told him I'd made a mistake, I wasn't in love with him, after all. The minute I met Alan I knew I'd never really been in love at all. Oh, I suppose you think I'm hopelessly light upon the weights, but when you're young you learn everything by trial and error, don't you?"

"What actually did you say? Come, Hatty, I'm your husband. If I'd actually seen you plant that knife between Miss Grey's shoulder-blades, I couldn't be put in the witness-box."

" I can't be expected to remember exactly what I said after all this time," declared Hatty, mutinous but undefeated. " Something about not meaning to let him spoil things between me and Alan."

" Was he threatening to do that ? "

" He rather fancied himself as John Savage's son-in-law. He wasn't particularly fond of work, and—he changed, Philip. During those last months . . ."

" After you met Duke ? "

" Yes. He showed me a side of himself I hadn't realised existed."

" Was there anything in that letter that could be construed as a threat ? Think before you answer."

" He was doing the threatening. He thought he could persuade Alan that there was much more to our relationship than was ever the case. Of course, I couldn't let him do that."

" If that particular letter had been produced at the inquest, would it have had any effect on a jury ? "

" How do I know how a jury's mind works ? "

" Much the same as any one else's. There was a threat in it ? "

" I said—so far as I remember—I'd see him dead before I'd let him spoil my life. A throw-back to the Victorian parent—I would sooner see you dead at my feet . . ."

" Don't lose your head," counselled her husband sharply. " We're in a spot and at the moment I don't quite see how things are going to work out."

" They've gone anyway," Hatty pointed out.

" That was just Chapter One. They'll be back. If only we could offer a molecule of proof that the car did break down. If you'd mentioned it to your mother . . ."

" No one knew I was expected early."

" No." His voice was unpromising.

" It doesn't have to be any of us," urged Hatty. " A girl like Marguerite Grey must have enemies all over the place."

Philip remembered a quotation that was one of Arthur Crook's favourites. " Some circumstantial evidence is very great, as when you find a trout in the milk."

" Oh," cried Hatty in a voice of desperation, " isn't it typical of her, that, after keeping me on tenterhooks all this time, she should go on being a danger to me even after she's dead."

Hilda West, having made and signed a statement at the police station, had a bad shock when her door-bell rang and she found Ferrers on the step.

" Dear me, do you suppose I can help you any further ? " she wondered, leading the way into her drawing-room—she had never grown accustomed to the modern word lounge. " But I suppose you have to cast your nets wide, leave no stone unturned."

" We don't really cast nets for stones," said Ferrers, " but we have to check up on every statement."

He'd seen everyone connected with the case, of course. Alison had repeated her story, and had produced an alibi ; a rude Lady Martin had stared at him as though he were a virus who could at least have gone round to the back door. Dacre and Dangerfield had been thrilled, and openly so, and only regretted they couldn't help more, but they'd been together all the morning and come in on the midday bus from shopping at Brightling. Mrs. Waltham had said, well, she didn't really know the dead girl well, she was rather a pushing type, look at the way she'd tried to winkle poor Miss West out of her shell.

" I understand she was a friend of Miss West's," the inspector had said, and Mrs. Waltham had muttered, " I wonder if that's the way Miss West regarded it."

All this was in the inspector's mind as he took the chair the old woman offered him, and watched her seat herself with her back to the light. He saw that she thrust her hands deep into the pockets of the rather shabby cardigan she wore over a dark dress that had seen the light a long time ago.

" Oh, how remiss ! " she exclaimed, jumping up again. " I never offered you anything to drink. I was going to have a—a little nip myself. My doctor has recommended a tablespoonful of brandy . . ."

She was all over the place, it was no wonder she jammed her hands in her pockets. It isn't only guilt that makes hands shaky.

"Well, not just for the moment," he said. "I shan't keep you very long. But seeing the dead girl was a friend of yours . . ."

"I don't know where you get your information from, Inspector, I'm sure I never told you that. She chose to regard me as an object of charity—such insolence."

"I suppose," said Ferrers, jumping for the opening like a clown going through a hoop, "the boot was never on the other foot?"

"Really, Inspector, I can't imagine what you mean."

"I mean, did she ever ask you for money?"

"It would have been quite absurd. I subsist, there is no other word for it, on a small annuity and a Government pension, it used to be called the Old Age Pension but now I believe it has been re-christened, like the workhouses that are now Twilight Homes or some such absurdity . . ." She stopped, panting. He was reminded of an old biddy he had seen only that morning, leading three lively terriers on strings, and being pulled all ways at once. "She had her little nip before I arrived," he reflected shrewdly, "and it wouldn't surprise me if it was more than one."

"I'm asking you a plain question, Miss West," he said. In his profession you were sunk if you let your heart rule your head. "Did Miss Grey ever ask you for money?"

"She had this refugee problem very much at heart. She wanted to raise an appreciable sum—oh, I don't wish to impugn her good motives, no one is wholly bad, and she said she could appreciate their position better than most, since for so many years she herself had had no home."

"That's not true, you know," Ferrers assured her. "Her father, a photographer in a small way, only died a few years ago, since when she looked after her mother and did some kind of work locally. It's only since Mrs. Grey's death that she's been at a loose end. And she seemed to have settled very comfortably with Miss Sheridan."

Miss West turned a ravished face towards him. " Why did Alison Sheridan put up with her ? What did she know ? She was a—a succubus . . ."

" Why was she asking you for money, Miss West ? "

" She thought it would be so nice if I could raise a sum, say, a hundred pounds, for the fund."

" What on earth made her think you might raise that amount ? "

" Oh, she had very grandiloquent ideas." She stumbled over the long word, but picked herself up quickly. " Naturally, I told her it was out of the question."

" And did she then let the matter drop ? "

" She had the impertinence to suggest that perhaps I could raise the amount from my nephew."

" Oh, you have a nephew ? "

" Oh, not in the neighbourhood, and naturally he has his own commitments. I seldom see him. When I was in the cottage hospital with pleurisy a year or two ago he came over from Seabrite—that is in Hampshire—but before then I had not seen him in—in a dog's age, as I think the young people say now."

" You're quite sure, Miss West, that Miss Grey wanted the money for the refugees ? "

" You're surely not suggesting that she was *dishonest* ? "

" I am asking you whether she asked for a contribution to her fund or whether she wanted the money for herself."

" Why on earth should she think I would give her money ? "

" There was no reason that you can suggest ? "

" Of course not."

" When she telephoned you on Wednesday morning, she said nothing about bringing any money with you ? "

" Certainly not. She simply said, ' Remember, I'm expecting you,' and rang off."

" You didn't take any appreciable sum of money with you ? "

" Inspector, I fail to see why I have to answer all these exceedingly personal questions. I have already told you it would be impossible for me to lay my hands on even so small a sum as fifty pounds, let alone a hundred."

" Did she utter any threats, Miss West, if you didn't produce the money ? "

" What could she threaten me with ? I didn't think she would pick up a poker and hit me over the head, and I disliked the girl, but I certainly cherished no murderous thoughts. And now may I ask a question ? Do you know who killed her ? "

" You'll hear the statement as soon as anyone else when we make one," Ferrers assured her.

After he had left the house he heard the trembling shooting of the bolt on the front door.

Henrietta came to see him that night. " I hear you've been calling on my daughter about the money Marguerite Grey was demanding. There's one point that perhaps you have overlooked. If Hatty wanted money, no matter how much, I could have supplied it. I shouldn't have had to tell her father, I needn't have spoken of it to anyone. I have my own income and my own bank account. In those circumstances, there could be no conceivable reason for her attacking the girl."

" We're not convinced this was a premeditated crime," Ferrers told her. " No weapon was brought to the scene, the murderer employed a knife belonging to Miss Sheridan, in a sense, you could say belonging to the deceased. We know Miss Grey had made an appointment with one member of the committee to come early, and had sent a telephone call to another."

" You only know that because they told you," Henrietta flamed.

" Oh, yes. The burden of proof is on us. We shan't move until we feel we have a case supported by the evidence."

" Which," said Henrietta furiously to her husband fortyeight hours later, when Ferrers again visited Bridge Street and this time didn't depart alone, " is all poppycock. They can't prove Hatty did it, and I understand she doesn't have to prove her innocence."

" It's not like you to shut your eyes to the obvious," said John Savage heavily. " She had means, motive and opportunity. Philip is going to London to see a man he knows who, he says, is unparalleled in cases like this one." And then suddenly his control broke, too. " Henry," he said, using a name he had disregarded for years and that went back to their courting days, " can you believe this is happening to our child ? "

Henrietta caught his arm. " I'm afraid, John. I wouldn't admit it to anyone but you, but—do you remember when she was only six years old and her dormouse died and the nurse wouldn't let her have a funeral but threw the body in the fire—Hatty went for her with a table-knife ? Oh, she didn't hurt her, but—no one could bring that up, could they ? "

" No one knows but ourselves, and I'd forgotten."

" If that Ferrers creature asks me if I ever knew her yield to violence I shall swear there was nothing—nothing. All this trouble started with Richard's death," she added in a quieter tone. " It's like a wheel and now it's come full circle. I never appreciated it before—the torture of the wheel, I mean."

It was a long time before he could calm her, and when later he went to telephone to his son-in-law he learned that he had already gone to London and might not be back that night.

CHAPTER X

THE CLOCK in Bloomsbury Terrace Square struck eight, an hour when honest men put by their work for the day. But Mr. Arthur Crook, that rogue elephant among lawyers, sat on in his eerie at 123 Bloomsbury Street, waiting for the unexpected. At ten minutes past eight his faith was justified. Feet rounded the corner of the stone staircase and climbed steadily towards his office.

It didn't occur to Crook that the owner of the footsteps could be looking for anyone except himself. For one thing, the rest of the offices had been closed for the better part of two hours, and for another, he occupied the whole of the top floor. Bill Parsons, his invaluable A.D.C., was out on some ploy or other, but Crook knew he wasn't the new-comer, because this man, whoever he might be, walked without a limp. When the footsteps paused at his door he leaped up and dragged it open.

" Welcome home," he said cheerfully, to the short, pale, dark-haired man he found waiting outside. A real fighter this, he decided, with a glow of satisfaction. They couldn't come too tough for him.

" Take a pew," he offered hospitably as Philip Cobb came in and stood looking round him in a rather dazed fashion. The state of the office would have made any tidy woman, like Alison Sheridan, for example, burst into tears. Newspapers were strewn everywhere, letters littered the heavy ink-stained desk, there were files on the uncomfortable chairs. Crook swept a few on to the floor, where there were already so many it made very little difference.

" So it's come," he said, flipping open the box of office cigarettes.

" Surely it's not in the papers yet ? " Philip sounded startled.

" Not unless they've put out a special edition, and you'd

have to be Royalty, or possibly Khrushchev, for that. Anyway, we know about these late-night finals. Buy 'em on the London streets at tea-time. When was it ? "

" Two—no, three hours ago. I suppose I was expecting it in a way, though disaster is always something that happens to the other chap, not to you."

" A slow learner," thought Crook compassionately. Surely he'd had time enough to accustom himself to the idea.

" No bail, of course," Philip went on, taking a cigarette and looking round as if he expected a lighter to fall out of the ceiling. Crook struck a wax vesta and obligingly held it out.

It occurred to Philip that Crook didn't seem in the least surprised to see him.

" You know who I am, then ? "

Crook dived to his right and picked up a newspaper from the mêlée on the floor.

" You take a nice picture," he congratulated him, displaying a photograph of Cobb getting into his car. " And don't worry about bail. It's best this way, really it is. If a chap's guilty then durance vile's the right place for him, and if he ain't he's often a lot safer behind bars than at loose. At least the real criminal can't get at him."

" I want to make it clear from the start," Philip said with a touch of truculence, " that I believe absolutely in my wife's innocence."

" Show me any husband that dares declare otherwise and I'll show you a candidate for the Gridiron Stakes," was Crook's prompt come-back. " Now, anything to add to what I know already ? "

" I take it you're aware of the circumstances."

" I know what the papers have printed. You got anything to tell me that ain't made the Press ? "

Philip hesitated, then told him about the incriminating letter.

" The day any dame's sent up for writing one lunatic letter, that's the day I turn in my cards," said Crook, cheerfully. " Now, anything else—strict confidence, of course. As the husband you can't be shoved in the witness-box.

Funny thing," he chatted on, giving his visitor an opportunity to pull himself together, " husbands pay the combined income tax, husbands are responsible for wives' debts, gas and electricity agreements are made out in their name, but when it comes to a murder charge they hardly count even as human beings."

" It's all deduction on the part of the police, of course, there's no direct evidence."

Crook nodded sympathetically. " Criminals are so unsporting, they won't commit their murders in public. Now, these letters. You knew about them ? "

" Only comparatively recently. Before then I'd merely realised that Miss Grey had some kind of unspecified hold over my wife. Otherwise, Hatty would never have agreed to serve on her committee."

" Not keen on playing second fiddle, I take it ? Well, who is ? "

" Sheridan told her he'd destroyed the lot and she believed him . . ."

" You're in the same racket as me," Crook warned him. " We both know nothing's evidence till it's been proved, and, Sheridan being dead, there's no chance of proof there. What you mean is, your wife says Sheridan told her he'd destroyed them."

" According to Miss Grey—and she spread this story pretty widely round the district—Sheridan wanted to marry her."

" See what I mean about proof ? " said Crook. " If he'd fallen for her, why keep his first love's letters ? "

" I can only think of one sound reason," Philip acknowledged.

" Two minds that think as one. Of course, they were the hold little Daisy-Bud had over Mrs. Cobb. Pity we don't know exactly what was in them, but we will."

" Can't we prevent their being offered in evidence ? "

" Proof of motive," Crook reminded him. " Still, look on the bright side, it may not come to evidence. What about the other members of the party ? "

" Miss West, who'll never see seventy again . . ."

"One of the most violent murderers I ever knocked up against was a frail old gentleman of eighty, who put three wives underground before he was nailed," said Crook, inelegantly. "How about the others?"

"Hatty's mother's out—she'd hire a jet plane to collect her girl from prison—three of the others, Dangerfield, Dacre and Waltham, all have alibis, and anyway no one can suggest a motive there. That leaves Lady Martin . . ."

"Anything known about her?"

"Husband was a boffin . . ."

"No little slip-ups, no secret letters to the Kremlin, anything Daisy-Bud might have uncovered?"

"I doubt it. In fact, I doubt if Lady M. would have given Miss Grey good morning if they'd met in the street, and if she had everyone would have known about it."

"Stronghold of the feudal system," approved Crook. "Good for them. There are times when I could do with a bit less democracy myself. By the way, make any efforts to get the letters back from Miss Grey?"

"No. I'm afraid I didn't regard them very seriously. I thought perhaps Hatty had expressed herself rather forcibly, but that they'd really only be of interest to a husband, so I thought that more or less spiked Miss Grey's guns. I was planning to take my wife north if I could get her to agree . . ."

"Women are born martyrs," Crook told him. "Why did she want to go on lying on her bed of nails?"

"She didn't see why a pack of loose-mouthed gossips should drive her out." Philip spoke with a ferocity that caused Crook to lift one thick red eyebrow. "She's very proud."

"You should have told her nothing would persuade you to budge and you'd have found her rarin' to go," said the cheerful cynic facing him. "Miss Grey didn't apply to you?"

"I'd have run her in for attempted blackmail if she'd put anything in writing," was Philip's hard retort.

"But Mrs. Cobb took her seriously, to the extent of

trying to raise enough money to ransom the correspondence. And she had a date with the dear departed . . ."

" Which she didn't keep."

" Which she alleges she didn't keep," Crook corrected him gently. " How did she go ? By car ? Yes, of course, that's her alibi, the car broke down. This house where the girl was found—something Cottage—isolated, would you say ? "

" It doesn't exactly stand in the middle of the Gobi Desert . . ."

" What I mean is, say the car had been standing in front of the house for, say, ten minutes, would it be likely to attract attention ? "

" That would depend on whether anyone passed," said Philip rather stupidly. " I suppose, though, it could have been parked at the back entrance. That isn't much more than a lane and it might easily escape notice by anyone coming along the road. But surely it's obvious this isn't a planned crime. The weapon alone . . ."

" It's the crimes that ain't planned that are the worst to solve," said Crook soberly. " If a chap's put down foundations he leaves a trail for you to follow. This way—well, anyone can snatch up a knife . . . Now, let's have the time-table."

He stopped drawing rows of the back views of cats with curling tails and bows round their necks, and dotted figures down on the back of an envelope.

11.30 Miss Sheridan leaves—that can be proved, because she caught her bus and reached her pub at about twelve or just before.

12.00 Mrs. Cobb gets her message from Marguerite Grey.

12.05 (say) Miss West ditto.

12.15 You ring your house and there's no answer.

12.45 Mrs. Savage and Miss West go into the house.

12.50 Discovery of body.

" Looks like death must have taken place between twelve-five and twelve-forty. Thirty-five minutes. Front door was open, anyone could have come in. Only—seeing Miss Grey was expecting Mrs. Cobb at twelve-thirty, it's hardly likely she'd have made a date with anyone earlier. Mrs. Cobb stickin' to her story about leavin' at twelve-fifteen ? "

" She must have left then, or she'd have been in when I telephoned. She'd never have let it ring unanswered."

" I didn't suppose she would," agreed Crook resignedly. " I can believe in unicorns and even fairies if I'm put to it, but not in a woman who'll let a phone ring its head off, not unless she's being held up in a corner by a jack-knife."

" No, she set out and her car broke down," Philip insisted. " That's what she's told the police, and that's what she's going to stick to."

Crook nodded despondently. " Sometimes," he said, " I despair of human nature, it's so plumb bone-headed. Like a lot of sheep, the human race. 'Can you prove you were not on the scene of the crime?' says Chief Inspector Slap-cabbage. 'Oh, no, officer, I couldn't have been because my car broke down, and nobody happened to come past.' Or, if they don't possess a car, it's, 'Oh, officer, I went to the pictures. I can tell you the name of the film and the stripper who figures in it.' Well, of course they can, and so could you or me if we took the trouble to walk past the cinema. Why can't they think up something new? 'To tell you the truth, officer, I was feeling lonely, so I picked up a girl and went home with her—no, I didn't ask her name and no, I don't remember the address, and it's no use expecting her to come forward because, of course, she shouldn't have been on the streets at all.' Now that's something like a story. Even if they could nail the girl the odds are about five hundred to one she wouldn't recognise the chap, any more than you could tell one cottage loaf from another. And you can take that prissy expression off your face. In our profession we can't expect only to rub shoulders with the *crème de la crème*. Soon be queueing for benefit if we did. Still, we've better fish to fry than red herrings. Do you suppose your wife had confided in anyone under the seal, as it were ? "

Cobb shook his head. " There was only her mother, and Mrs. Savage would have gone round and paid Miss Grey out of hand if she'd known what was cooking."

" I see," said Crook. " Now, when you see your wife again, tell her she can stop worrying because my clients are always innocent, they have to be if I'm to eat. And if she's got anything up her sleeve beside her arm tell her to shake it down for my benefit. Ever hear of Artemus Ward ? "

" Well, of course."

" No of course about it. Lots of chaps of your age think he's a footballer who didn't quite make the grade. He said something every lawyer could stick over his desk. First get your evidence, then arrange it any way you please. Only— you've got to get your evidence ; so you warn Mrs. C. it never pays to renege on your friends, and at the moment I'm the best friend she's got. By the way," he was glancing back over the few notes he had made, " what caused you to ring your wife at twelve-fifteen ? "

" Oh, to warn her I shouldn't be back to lunch. I usually go home if I've no other appointment."

" Something come up suddenly ? "

" A client of ours, a Colonel Anstruther, a cripple since he had a stroke—I had to get his signature to some papers that had been delayed and Arbuthnot thought it would be a good idea to go along in person."

" What's Beggar's Alley like ? Is there a garage handy ? "

" It's like its name. More or less derelict. I can't think really why she went that way, except that she may have thought she was running it fine and wanted to get her business with Miss Grey settled before anyone else turned up."

" Ever been in the Hampton Court Maze ? " inquired Crook. " I was once. Forty times I came back to the centre. In the end the chap had to get on to his platform and give me instructions through a megaphone. We must hope Providence has its megaphone handy for us now. Y'see, it's statements, statements, all the way and not a ha'porth of proof. Still, I've been in a fair number of culs-de-sac in my time and mostly if you can't climb over the wall you can batter your way through."

He moved, indicating that as far as he was concerned, the interview was over. " Now, remember," he warned Philip, who seemed disposed to stop there and mull over the situation all night, " you've handed me the baby, you leave it to me to dandle it and tuck it up and give it its bottle. I'm known as one of the best baby-minders in the business and the chaps who'd cry aye to that would surprise you."

Hatty had lost colour and weight since the trouble began, but she was still beautiful enough to make that unromantic old shark, Arthur Crook, gasp at his first sight of her. Not, to do him justice, that it made any difference to his attitude. He'd have worked just as zestfully for a female with a face like the back of a taxi-cab. Only it did make you realise she'd have a lot of enemies. If your friends feel more kindly disposed to you when you're a failure, as Oscar Wilde is said to have declared, he hadn't a doubt that women loved their neighbours better when they were plainer than themselves.

" My husband told me to expect you," said Hatty, composedly, as if she· were welcoming him to her own drawing-room. " I ought to warn you, though, that I can't tell you any more than I've told the police, and if they don't believe my story why should they believe yours ? "

" Oh well," said Crook cosily, " it might sound a bit different coming from me. And I don't gather you were exactly forthcoming about the letters."

" I didn't have to be. They told me."

" That's the police all over. What was so deadly about them, anyway ? Any indication you'd been putting the cart before the horse, where young Sheridan was concerned, I mean ? "

She looked at him, not in indignation, but in amazement.

" Well, of course not. Why should we ? I was of age, I could have married him at any time, only—it's rather odd, but though I really was in love with him once I never remember contemplating being Mrs. Richard Sheridan. There was something—and how right I was," she wound up, with sudden vigour.

"Middle name not precisely Galahad?" suggested Crook, who had nearly been christened Galahad himself.

"It was after I told him I'd changed, then he began to show the cloven hoof. Though even then I hadn't realised he'd kept the letters."

"Threatened to have a word on the strict q.t. with swain number two? How about him, by the way?"

"Oh, that was different again." Her first composure had given place to something a great deal more flattering to her visitor. A kind of confidence that made him think, I shall end up the cosy family lawyer yet. "I'd have married Alan at the drop of a hat."

"Only—he kept it on his head?"

Hatty nodded. "I quite thought he wouldn't let it make any difference. How wrong can you be?"

Crook let that one ride. "When did you know the letters hadn't gone into the garbage can?"

"When Marguerite Grey started quoting from them. She'd found them or he'd given them to her, I don't know which, and I suppose now, since they're both dead, I shall never know. Perhaps he thought, so long as he had them, he could stop me marrying Alan."

"You seem to have had a let-off there," suggested Mr. Crook candidly.

"Oh, I always knew there was something—at least during these last few months."

"Since he met little Daisy-Bud?"

Hatty considered. "I'm not sure exactly when he did meet her, but it might be that. But—I don't suppose you can understand—everything at home seemed so safe, you could plan and know it would all work out right, because even Providence had to go Father's way. He—Richard— seemed to come out of another world, and—oh, he fascinated me."

"So do cobras, I'm told. Never met any myself. What made you marry Cobb?"

For the first time she seemed disconcerted. " Why, he asked me."

" So had various other chaps, I gather. What made you pick him ? "

" Ah, but he was the only one—afterwards. Women appreciate that kind of thing."

" No offers before the catastrophe ? "

She said quite carelessly, " I suppose he knew he wouldn't have a chance."

" Not the first time an Also Ran pulled off a big race," said Crook in his insensitive way.

"Women . . ." Hatty began, but he interrupted her. " Don't start trying to teach me anything about women, I'd as soon start studying Choctaw. Well, he was handy and willing and you didn't have to put up a front with him. . . . When did you tell him about the letters ? "

" I let it out by accident—after the marriage. I didn't mean to tell him about them at all ; why, at that time I didn't realise they still existed. It was after Marguerite Grey came to call. . . ."

" Why not tell him the whole story ? "

" Even husbands have feelings," flashed the girl.

" Dynamite, eh ? " Crook suggested.

" It would depend who was reading them. The police . . ."

" They are human," said Crook surprisingly. " Obviously they'd take the perfect sacrificial victim when she's offered them on a plate. Still, it wouldn't surprise me if little Daisy-Bud had her knife into quite a lot of other folk. Trouble with blackmailers is they ain't got imagination, never seems to occur to them someone might reverse the process and leave them at the receiving end. Like a T.B. carrier, wherever she goes she carries the deadly seed."

" It could be someone we don't know."

" It could. Only that someone would have to know about the fork luncheon and the house being empty—unless you're going to try and pin this on little old coincidence. Got any particular enemies ? " he added, with no particular change of voice.

" Not now Marguerite's gone."

" Well, the one thing I do know is she didn't stick the knife between her own shoulder-blades. So there has to be someone, if we're to follow that line. Anyone sweet on Mr. Galahad Cobb ? Or wouldn't you know ? "

" So far as I'm concerned, his life, before he married me, was a closed book, on the personal plane, I mean. I don't think anyone knows much about him."

" A lot of people are probably going to be surprised to realise how much they know before the curtain drops," Crook assured her. " It could even be that little Daisy-Bud was doing a bit of boasting round about and X got to hear about it and remembered the one about silence being golden. The number of murders that should be tagged suicide would surprise you." He stood up, brisk and bouncing. " End of the first lesson," he said. " If you think of anything else that could stand up to cross-examination, make a note of it and let me have it next time I come. Y'know, it wouldn't be the first time a little greedy-guts had tried to work a double take and come to grief in the process."

CHAPTER XI

AT THE DUCK AND GREEN PEAS they turned out to gawp at Crook's vintage yellow Rolls, the Old Superb, when he brought her to a standstill in the diminutive car-park. When they'd had an eyeful of her they looked at Crook himself, and that filled the other eye. He came marching into the bar like a man at the head of an invisible band and asked for a pint, that he put down at a single swallow. This at once enlisted the potman on his side. Any chap who can dispose of beer in this fashion is worthy of respect. Mrs. Groves came in while he was there and he bought her a couple of black velvets. Nothing like your favourite tipple for loosing the tongue, was one of his mottoes.

" That Miss Grey ! " sniffed Mrs. Groves. " Thought herself the cat's whiskers, and who was she, when all's said and done ? Selling gloves behind a counter in a place like Bootles—clock in, clock out and never speak out of turn. A proper slave. It's no wonder she did a bit of slave-driving herself when she moved into the cottage."

" Eased you out pretty quick, didn't she ? " insinuated Mr. Crook.

" I could have had the law on her only I wouldn't demean myself."

" Quite right," approved Crook. " Fill up the lady's glass again, George. Some risks you may have to take, get yourself sent on a rocket to the moon, go bathing in a shark pond, if that's your fancy, and you might stand a chance, if your teeth are good enough, but stay away from lawyers."

" That's funny advice, seeing you call yourself one," said Mrs. Groves admiringly, receiving her third glass.

" Nothing to what other chaps call me, including the police. Ever open up—Miss Grey, I mean—let on what she was doing before she came here ? "

" Lived in the country somewhere, I b'lieve, selling something else, I wouldn't wonder. Picked up Mr. Richard—he was what you might call . . ." she rootled round in her mind for the appropriate word.

" Suggestible ? "

" Mind you, I never believed he was going to marry her."

" Maybe she wouldn't have agreed. There was that hundred pounds, remember."

" He never give her that. He never had a hundred pounds in his natural. Why, he borrowed off of me more than once. Mind you, he had a way with him, difficult to refuse, if you get my meaning."

" Handsome is as handsome does, and it does a lot of people I know. Miss Sheridan kind of fell for him, too, I understand ? "

" Oh well, he was her nephew, that was different. Thought the world of him she did, and twist her round his little finger, he could. But after he come of age, well, she seemed more worried-like, afraid he might take himself off, I suppose."

" Marry Miss Savage, for example ? "

" Well, he had something in mind. He told me as much."

" I seem to remember he told a few other people." He clenched his big fist. " I've got her like that, in the hollow of my hand—isn't that what he said ? Well, if he had those letters everyone's talking about . . ."

" Mind you," repeated Mrs. Groves, " I wouldn't have bothered to go to church with him myself. Nice as pie so long as everything went all right, but—he reminded me of my brother-in-law. One of the handsomest chaps you ever set eyes on, but he cracked my sister's skull with a beer bottle two years after they were wed."

" Perhaps," suggested Crook, diffidently, " she was an aggravating woman."

" Oh, she was," acknowledged Mrs. Groves handsomely, " but if we were all to go round cracking skulls because people were aggravating, they wouldn't have enough prisons to house us."

" Never happened to mention Miss Grey to you, I take it ? "

" Not a word. She popped up like a Jack-in-the-box, well, Jill-in-the-box, I suppose I should say. Got her claws into him, I shouldn't wonder. Well, look at the way she's dug herself in. That poor old Miss West. What I say is, if the drink's a comfort you've no right, not if you call yourself a Christian, to go depriving folk."

" And that's what she was trying to do ? Wean the old lady off the bottle ? "

" Now, if she'd been the one that was being threatened, she might have shelled out a hundred pounds, if she'd had it, only she wouldn't either."

Crook thought that if the recording angel ever wanted any help he could do worse than go into a huddle with such as Mrs. Groves ; there wasn't much they missed.

" All the same, I wonder if she knows quite everything here," he told himself, buying them both a final glass and taking himself off. He knew, none better, that sex and age

and the state of your health have much less to do with the
commission of murder than the man in the street would
believe.

Henrietta was preparing to go out to a meeting of the
Parochial Church Council when Mr. Crook blew in. Blew
was the operative word ; the pictures trembled on the walls,
and the ornaments jumped on the mantelpiece. Crook looked
at them with approval. He liked a room that was cluttered
according to modern notions. "All that extra dusting," Hatty
said scornfully. "Walls 'ull be bare enough in the grave,"
opined Mr. Crook, " and what's a little dust anyway ? "

Henrietta was less composed than her daughter. Nothing
Philip Cobb had told her had prepared her for this red-
headed giant—it came as a shock after they had been talking
for some time to realise he was slightly below average height,
so bulky did he seem—with his atom-bomb tactics.

" Your daughter apart," said Crook, " who's your bet for
the murder stakes ? "

" I hadn't thought." She seemed dumbfounded.

" Think now," Crook offered.

" If it has to be someone we know there are only about
six possibles and none of them seem to fit the bill."

" How about an old pet called West ? The lady cleaner
in the pub . . ."

" I do hope, Mr. Crook, you've not been listening to
gossip." The words broke from Henrietta before she could
stop them.

Crook looked genuinely amazed. " Unless you're sittin'
on some proof, what else have I got to go on ? " he demanded. " Mrs. Groves . . ."

" A most unreliable woman. What did she tell you about
Hatty ? "

" My client ? Oh, we didn't discuss her. She seems to
think there's some tie-up between Miss West and the late
unlamented."

" What did she say ? "

Crook went through a graphic pantomime of tilting the
elbow.

" Nonsense ! " declared Henrietta, with more violence

than the occasion appeared to warrant. " I've lived here for twenty-five years and I've never seen Miss West the worse for drink."

" See much of her ? "

" Not a great deal. She keeps herself to herself as they say. Not at all well off, I understand."

" Price of drink's a scandal," her visitor concurred. " Still, you had heard the rumour."

" People will say anything."

" No one has told me you take a bottle to bed, so why Miss West ? Besides, you didn't answer my question."

" I can't see that it has any bearing on the point at issue."

" O.K.," said Crook. " You had heard the rumour and no question about it, it wasn't a secret to Mrs. G. By this time it can't be a secret to anyone else who happened to be in the Duck at lunch-time to-day. Well, if you'd ever tried your hand at blackmail—I'm sure you haven't—you'd know you can't expect to winkle money out of your victims by threatenin' to spread abroad a story that's common knowledge anyway. Ergo, there was something else. No notion what it might be, I suppose ? "

" About Miss West ? Of course not. I can't help feeling you're mistaken, Mr. Crook."

" I never met little Daisy-Bud but the mould once made wasn't broken, and I've been meeting her twin sisters for the last thirty years. She wouldn't bother over an old woman unless there was something in it for her. What started her off ? She didn't know Miss West before she came here, Marguerite Grey, I mean ? "

" I can't imagine it."

" That's another funny thing. No one seems to know anything about the girl. Mrs. Groves supposes she'd worked in a shop in her native county. What was Richard Sheridan doing down there anyway ? "

" If you'd asked me what hold Marguerite had over Miss Sheridan I might have been able to tell you—unless she's already told you herself."

" I haven't seen her yet," Crook confessed. " She don't surface till the evening, and I don't fancy going along to that pub she runs. Might find myself doing a St. Lawrence on the gridiron." He looked down at his plump rotundities.

Henrietta bit back a chuckle; goodness knows, there hadn't been much to laugh at lately.

" Almost hear the fat sizzle, can't you ? " Crook agreed. " According to Mrs. G., Miss Sheridan was devoted to her nephew."

" I don't think there can be any doubt about that; and she was horrified when Marguerite Grey suddenly put in an appearance. It was as much of a shock to her as to anyone."

" Richard not having mentioned her ? "

" I was at the inquest when Marguerite surfaced, as you'd say, and I swear it was as much of a surprise to Alison as it was to the rest of us."

" And the lady claimed she and Richard were secretly plighted—something of that kind ? "

" I don't think anyone believed her."

Crook smote his two big hands together. " It's like living in a world of culs-de-sac," he said. " But you were going to tell me how he met her and what her hold was over Auntie."

" If you've never lived in the country, Mr. Crook, you can't appreciate how gossip spreads and the harm it can do. It's like dropping a lighted match in a forest. No one notices it much at first, and suddenly the whole place is ablaze."

She told him quite simply what Alison had recounted to her.

" Any possibility that the lady did know which kid she'd grabbed ? " asked Crook. " I mean, you can't by-pass human nature, and if the two of them were cluttered up together . . ."

" In that case, I think she'd have tried to rescue both. She mightn't have succeeded, but at least there would be evidence that she had tried. And I don't think she would have abandoned the orphan and gone back for Richard, if it had been that way round."

" Only it wasn't. Still, it's a whale of a time ago."

" That wouldn't stop people's tongues, particularly now Richard is dead. A judgment, they might say—you've no notion how blasphemous pious people can be—she pounced on the one who meant her living—because that's what it was under her brother's will—and let the other one take his chance. A story like that could be blown up into something quite poisonous. After all, my dear, we know the poor little thing must have been an expense to her, because the mother never even sent clothes, and he had bad blood and might have turned out a bad bargain—and there was the point that the authorities didn't let the little girls go back to her— well, she says the parents reclaimed one and the local council found a foster-mother for the other—it could be made to sound quite dangerous."

" Especially served up with a bit of malice the way Daisy-Bud would dish it up. A hint about howls coming from a dark cupboard, something nasty seen in the wood-shed— and, of course, no parents to ask questions. What I don't quite get is where Marguerite Grey comes in."

" She knows something about Richard—Alison admitted as much."

" Such as ? "

" She wouldn't say. But Marguerite got a hundred pounds out of him, and we still don't know where it came from."

" Not his bank account ? "

Henrietta shook her head. " You didn't know Richard. Hatty's bad enough, but spending money was like a disease with him."

" Sure she didn't lend him a hand ? "

" She says not and I believe her."

" Might have had collateral ? " Crook suggested.

" The only things she had of any value she tried to sell off to keep Marguerite quiet. Besides, why should she be giving Richard money ? She didn't realise he had kept the letters. You've seen her, of course. Was she—unbearably difficult ? "

" You know what they say about the primrose path," Crook reminded her.

" Oh well, I hope you can cope. It's a tough assignment."

" Know who I never had any sympathy for ? " Crook
asked her. " The toad beneath the harrow. It should either
have got out of the harrow's way like a bat out of hell, or
got up on its hindlegs and put up a fight. How does anyone
know harrows ain't cowards at heart ? It had a chance of
making history, but no, it lay down and let itself be mashed."

" Well, certainly no one could think of you as a toad,"
said Henrietta. " I wish I could be of more use. There's
an idea, fostered, I'm certain by men, that girls confide in
their mothers . . ."

" Don't strip all my illusions from me," Crook begged.
" I'll be naked to every wind without that and think what a
scandal that 'ud be. Coming back to Miss West, can you
think of anyone who'd know her a bit better than you ? "

" I believe she has a nephew but they're on distant terms.
Here—I doubt it. And yet I got the impression that day
she longed for a friend, a confidante."

" This is the day of the murder you're talking about ? "

" That's right. As a matter of fact, we had more conversation that day than we'd had in the previous twelve
months. We met on the step and she was nervous about
going up alone."

" Not wanting to find herself *tête-à-tête* with little Miss
Grey ? "

" Perhaps. In fact, I got the impression she wanted to
avoid seeing her in any case. She made some excuse, she'd
forgotten her gloves and I believe she'd have run home
and got them, but I wouldn't let her, because I thought
she mightn't come back."

" Why come in the first place ? "

" I don't think she had any choice. From all I've heard,
I should say Marguerite was quite an adept at cracking the
whip."

" She didn't say anything while you waited about before
the others came that could help us at all ? Just a hint . . ."

Henrietta shook her head. " She made small talk, about
bazaars—she was quite an adept at them in her young days,
her father had been a canon, and of course she'd never gone
out to earn a living, sat about and embroidered and made

traycloths—oh, the rubbish you used to be expected to buy at bazaars in those days. I remember going with my mother sometimes—all such deserving causes and at Christmas we'd go through the things we'd bought and see if we dared send this one to one relative and that to another—as she said, nobody would have dared send a cubist canvas, if that's what it was . . ."

Mr. Crook looked puzzled. " What what was ? "

" Oh, there was a frightful monstrosity propped up against the table behind the curtain with all the other things— Marguerite had assembled them all, goodness knows why, no one was going to do any shopping that afternoon—and vases, the new kind that are made for flowers to fall out of. It was all very small change, just passing the time really. And then Hatty came in. It was quite a relief. I was running out of small talk."

" Ah yes, Hatty. Now, you're dead sure she didn't say anything about the car breaking down and that making her late ? "

" We didn't know she was late. We had been invited for one o'clock and she arrived about ten to. For Hatty, that was a miracle. Then the others drifted in and still no Marguerite, and at last someone thought perhaps she was playing a practical joke and someone—one of the Danger-field-Dacre pair, I think—pulled back the curtain. And even then for the first few seconds we didn't realise what had happened—the shawl hid the haft of the knife—and it was Mrs. Waltham who began to scream."

" Where were all the others ? "

" Hatty was standing by the fireplace, I think—she seemed cold and there was a huge electric fire burning— Lady Martin was by the table, you could see her calculating to a penny what everything had cost—Miss West was by the window, looking out, she was the only one who didn't see what had happened, not till Mrs. Waltham screamed ; she was watching for Marguerite, we thought she might be out . . ."

" Oh, well," said Crook, " maybe that's country manners. She didn't faint or anything ? "

"Nobody fainted. Lady Martin was quite capable of slapping anyone's face who even suggested it. Miss West was just saying, 'I don't see any sign of her,' when the curtain was pulled back, Mrs. Dacre gave a sort of giggle, that's the nearest anyone came to hysteria . . . I'm sorry, Mr. Crook. I'd help you more if I could. I believe I'd hang this murder round anyone's neck if it would clear Hatty."

"That's my girl," said Crook warmly. "And don't fret. You've done fine, just fine. Now, about the others? Got their addresses?"

Henrietta supplied them. "Though I don't see how any of them can help you much, because Hilda West and I were there when they arrived."

"Well, the one I want is the one who got there before you. In my racket, you learn the truth of the text that not one sparrow falls to the ground unnoticed and it certainly don't when Arthur Crook's around. Why, I've known cases where just one sentence from a character who's hardly in the picture has unlocked the whole puzzle."

"Well," said Henrietta, turning up a local map to show him how best to reach the various houses he intended to visit, "I do hope you've brought your bullet-proof waistcoat with you, because I have an idea you're going to need it."

"My strength is as the strength of ten for reasons I needn't underline," Crook assured her. "Lady Martin likely to have her knife into the little girl?"

"Oh, it can't have been her. She'd come by car—she even takes it to go to church and that's only about five minutes from her door. But you could check with Palmer, her chauffeur. And the Dacre-Dangerfield combination came in together on the bus, and anyone else on board would testify to them. You can't overlook them. Mrs. Waltham— she'll have come by car, too, I should think."

"How about this Miss West? Where does she hang out?"

"Beddoes Lane. Quite a small turning; the houses were all cottages once."

"Costing three hundred pounds, now prettified and put

on the market at three thousand pounds, with dry-rot thrown in," amplified Crook rapidly.

" There's a drinking fountain in it christened by George IV. It's on the map. I'll show you."

Crook bent his big red head over the map she produced. " She'd come up Anson Street," he decided, " or does she come by car, too ? "

" Not by car," was Henrietta's sedate reply.

" And you ? "

" Oh, I walked."

" So you should have met in the middle."

" We would have done if I had started out earlier. As it was, she was on the doorstep. She'd rung three times, she said."

" The time being . . . ? "

" Twelve-forty-five. I wanted a word with Marguerite."

" Any use asking what about ? "

" Hatty," said Henrietta simply. " I didn't know she had the letters, but I knew she had something."

Crook nodded and looked round for his hat, from which he had refused to be parted in the hall. " I'll be on my way," he said. " Now, don't look so downcast. You're the first ray of light I've seen. Now I'll really get started. Labourer is worthy of his hire, but he has to earn it, and that's a thing the Welfare State don't seem to have taught as many people as they might. But there," he continued benevolently, jamming the hat on the back of his head, " I expect you're like all the high and mighty since the war, vote on a red ticket. I was never educated up to Labour." He prepared to charge out, like a bull through a china shop ; Henrietta could almost hear the tinkle of broken plates.

On her way back from the quarter of the Parish Church Council meeting that she had attended, Henrietta ran into old Miss West. Hilda was clearly in a state.

" I hear that Mr. Crook has been to see you," she said, twisting her fingers miserably. " Did he say anything about coming to me ? "

" He asked for your address," admitted Henrietta. " But

I shouldn't worry about him. He's a kitten, he is really."
(Crook would probably have succumbed to apoplexy if he
could have heard her.)

" What sort of things did he ask you ? "

" Chiefly about that last day when we found Marguerite's
body. I couldn't tell him anything. I said we'd gone up
together."

" I can't help him. Did you say that ? "

Henrietta considered. " I don't think he's the kind of
person you tell things to, I mean in the sense of instructing.
But he'll probably make the rounds, like the police. Oh,
come, you've nothing to be afraid of."

Miss West lifted her trembling face. " You don't know
Norman, he's my nephew. He holds a very important
position in a government department. Violet always says I
wouldn't understand and I don't ask any questions, but
he was seriously put out when he heard the police had been
asking questions, and he'll be worse still when he hears a
private detective has been to see me."

" Mr. Crook isn't a private detective, he's a lawyer, and
he's only trying to find out the truth about Marguerite's
death."

" Mrs. Savage, you know I would help him if I could
but I can tell him nothing, nothing. Of course, I do see it's
dreadful for you—poor Hatty ! Does he think he can
help ? "

Henrietta said, before she thought what she was going to
say, " Well, of course he'll help. He's the kind of person
that never loses because he doesn't believe he can. What an
extraordinary thing to say," she ran on, before Miss West
could make any comment. " I've only just realised that.
Now, my dear, do stop worrying, there's nothing for you to
lose your sleep over. And if it's Norman," she added un-
controllably, " I can assure you, Mr. Crook is more than
a match for a dozen Normans, and their Violets thrown
in."

Miss West gave her a weak, apologetic smile and seemed
to vanish like the Cheshire Cat's grin. One minute she was
there, the next she wasn't. Henrietta felt quite shaken. She

would have been more shaken still if she could have seen Hilda West a little later, sitting in her Victorian drawing-room, her arms draped in a lilac cardigan folded over her thin chest, her face as white as her white hair, swaying to and fro as if to some ghostly tune and muttering to herself.

" He mustn't find out," she said. " Why should he ? No one knows except me, and I shan't tell. Of course, lawyers are very cunning, but no one can have told him because no one else knows. I'll just stick to that, if he should come. ' I can't say anything. I don't know anything.' If I just cling to those two sentences I must be all right."

Because she couldn't convince herself and so, naturally, didn't suppose she'd be able to convince Mr. Crook, she had recourse to the brandy bottle from which she had so strenuously striven to wean herself, and when the telephone did ring about 9.30 she didn't answer it, because she didn't hear.

And if Henrietta would have been shocked to know how Miss West spent her evening, the old woman herself would have been dumbfounded to realise where Crook was spending his. The rumour went round the Duck and Green Peas and The Leather Bottel that he'd pulled out already, there was a London chap all over, so impatient, never stopped to ask them as might be able to help. . . . The Dangerfield-Dacre connection got wind of the story—they'd made their husbands take them up to the Leather Bottel to collect the dirt they said, in their bright slangy way, and when they heard he'd gone, they were furious.

" Without even seeing us ? " they fumed.

" What could you have told him ? " their innocent husbands inquired.

They stared at the creatures in scorn. They couldn't have told Crook anything, of course, but that wouldn't have stopped them talking. Class distinction, they decided, that's what it was. He'd been to see Henrietta, hadn't he ? He'd even talked to the daily woman. Oh well—they signalled imperiously to their husbands for a fill-up of gin and lime—if he paid any attention to her he couldn't be much good.

While Miss West was still sitting helplessly by her fireside wondering what on earth would happen if trouble reached Norman's ears, Arthur Crook was rolling across two counties to see that Norman West who occupied all his aunt's thought. There had been no difficulty in discovering his whereabouts. Hilda had spoken of Seabrite in Hampshire and the telephone directory did the rest. It was eight o'clock when he arrived, and Violet West had just served coffee in the lounge in fiddling little cups with purple borders. When Crook rang and knocked, Norman himself glanced out of the window, and instantly assumed the visitor had come to the wrong house. No one owning that out-of-date monstrosity could possibly be an acquaintance of his. But when Crook rang again he came pompously into the hall and opened the door a few inches. Crook with the expertness of long practice thrust a large brown shoe into the aperture.

" We don't buy at the door," said the man, who had a square face about as soft as a lump of teak, with a buttoned-up mouth and small, roving eyes.

" O.K. by me," agreed Crook. " I've got nothing to sell."

" And we don't give either."

" I believe you, brother."

" Then you've come to the wrong house."

" Name of West ? " asked Crook.

" Well ? "

An invisible voice called out, " What is it, Norman ? " and Norman answered testily, " I can deal with it. Now . . ." he turned back to Crook.

" Next-of-kin to Miss Hilda West of Burlham, Mereshire ? "

The nephew fell back in sheer astonishment, and when he'd come round from that he found the interloper was in the hall.

" What—what has happened to my aunt ? She's not . . ."

" I haven't come from the undertakers," Crook promised.

" Then—the police ? "

Crook's expressive red brows rose. " Expecting them ? "

" Of course not."

" I know what it is," said Crook. " You're thinking I look like a retired super."

" I know nothing about the appearance of police officers, in or out of uniform," said Norman sourly. " And if you do not represent them . . ."

" But you've been expecting me or someone like me," Crook told himself shrewdly. He produced one of his preposterous professional cards. " Acting for the defence in the murder of Marguerite Grey," he explained.

" I fail to see how that concerns my aunt . . ."

" You will," Crook promised. " Look, I charge by time . . ."

"'Then I can promise you you will have no reason to present a bill on my account," retorted Norman West swiftly. " My aunt is not concerned . . ."

" Only up to her chin. Tell me, Mr. West, why was she being blackmailed ? "

" Who says . . . ? " But a pudgy hand came out and caught stealthily at the ledge of a table set against the wall. " Blackmailed, indeed."

" I do," Crook assured him, " and if you're goin' to repeat everything I say you'd do better to keep a tame parrot."

This rudeness was so gross that Norman found he had opened the door of what he called the library—though all his reading was confined to the financial columns of the Press and you don't need a whole room just for that—and both men had passed in.

" I take it you have evidence my aunt was being—that demands were being made on her ? " demanded Norman, who looked even less appetising at closer quarters.

" Well, I don't think she cottoned on to dear little Marguerite because she reminded her of her own youth or anything like that," Crook assured him. " Had it ever happened before ? "

" Certainly not. And you've yet to convince me it has happened now."

The door of the library opened and a hard-faced biddy looked in. You could sow a crop of mustard and cress in the stuff she'd plastered on her moniker, reflected Mr. Crook, who didn't like women much anyway, but definitely preferred them with clean faces.

" Oh, Norman," lied the apparition, " I didn't realise you were engaged. Your coffee's getting cold."

" No coffee for me," said Crook swiftly. He hadn't much hope he was going to be offered anything stronger. He came to his feet with one of his alligator grins, Little Lord Fauntleroy in his maturity. " Don't go, ma'am. Maybe you could help us. In my experience the ladies tend to hang together."

" It's about Aunt Hilda, Vi," her husband said, and anything less like a violet you couldn't imagine.

" Are you a doctor ? "

" The Health Service has changed overnight if you suppose doctors come traipsing across two counties to see nextof-kin. When we have the noble police and the telephone . . ." He turned to Norman. " You'll be having a crop of slander actions on your hands if you're not careful," he warned him. " First the police, now the medical profession —neither of them would touch me with a barge-pole."

" Mr. Crook believes that Aunt Hilda is being blackmailed."

" Then why hasn't she gone to the police ? "

" Maybe you'd like me to get them for you," offered Crook.

" What is it this time ? " demanded Violet ungraciously.

Her husband flapped an unavailing hand in her direction, but the cat was out of the bag by now.

" Bit of trouble heretofore ? " Crook inquired, big brown eyes a-gleam.

" I still fail to understand why you are here. Even the police can hardly be suggesting that my aunt has any connection with the murder of this unfortunate young woman."

" On the spot when the body came to light," Crook

reminded him. " How long has your auntie been livin' in Burlham ? "

" About thirty years. She nursed an invalid mother . . ."

" And during the last ten years, say, any notion how often she's been outside the house and into someone else's ? "

" I understand she lives very quietly."

" Not any more," Crook murmured.

" Can't you come to the point ? " demanded Violet brutally. " Or are you here just to stir up a bit of mud ? "

" Of course not." That was Norman, his voice as agitated as a prawn's whisker. " No one could wish to harm an old lady . . ."

" You didn't know Daisy-Bud," said Crook. " And she ain't that old."

" Age is more than a matter of years. And when the person concerned has a—a weakness . . ."

" So you do know about it ? " Crook was openly amazed.

" Naturally we know. My husband and I have had the responsibility . . . We have done everything in our power to persuade Miss West to enter some institution where she would have a little friendly surveillance . . ."

" Like a padded cell, say ? "

" Certainly not. But—she does require supervision. I would have suggested her coming here, but we have two sons of our own and we have to consider their future. Gossip flies like a bird."

" Messy things birds," Crook agreed.

" And no one can suggest it is a—a criminal tendency . . ."

"Well, I should hope not." Crook looked honestly shocked, recalling presumably the half million or so of beer bottles littering his personal past. " It's all a matter of the age you live in. There was a time when all the nobility suffered from the same weakness . . ."

Norman seemed to have decided a little civility wouldn't come amiss. He doled it out as a mean man doles out coppers. " It's not as though she ever needs the things she takes," he explained earnestly. " They seemed to be—er—

picked up at random. Her own home is adequately furnished
with all necessities, and if there was anything else she did
require—well, she is not without relatives."

" 'Unto each man his burden, unto each his crown,' "
quoted Crook, rapidly, " only the burden is generally more
in evidence." And he reflected that having relatives didn't
help much if their doorbell didn't work and their telephone
was permanently out of order, when you rang up.

" I have actually discussed this—er—tendency with an
alienist," Norman ploughed on. " Nowadays, when free
treatment is available under the National Health Act . . .
He was an excellent man. He spoke of the laws of compensation."

" For Auntie? I'd have thought the other side were the
ones for that. Now, let's have it in words of one syllable."
He reflected he'd learned practically all he'd come to know
without asking a single question. " Your auntie hasn't had
much fun out of life, unpaid nurse for twenty years, so she
gets her own back by nicking the spoons when she goes out
to tea. That about the size of it ? "

" Kleptomania is as much a disease as—as a tendency to
asthma," put in the detestable Violet. " As I said before, it
has been a great anxiety to us for a considerable time."

" But not enough for you to offer her a home here. No,
don't give me the one about your sons again. They sound
to me a pair of sissies if they can't stand up to one old
lady. Besides, if she had a place in society she might find
that more of a compensation than spoons she don't want.
She's been writing to you for money, maybe ? " he added
to Norman.

" I told you there was something wrong," declared
Violet. " Naturally I never supposed she needed a hundred
pounds to give to a charity. Oh dear, I did hope after last
time . . ."

" When was that ? " asked Crook.

" Rather more than two years ago there was a most unfortunate incident. Luckily my husband, who is not without
influence, was able to—er—hush the matter up."

" I felt I must warn my aunt that any repetition would

result in my being compelled to ask for a medical certificate,"
pontificated Norman.

" Got a tame medico in your pocket, I suppose. What
was your idea ? I understand these nursing homes are a bit
pricey."

Norman and his spouse exchanged telling glances. How
such a bounder ever found his way into the Law List,
search them.

" There could be no question of a private home," Norman
replied stiffly. " Miss West's income is exceedingly limited
—an annuity, in short . . ."

" So she'd either have to go free or to some third-rate
place where, every time a postage stamp was missing, all
eyes 'ud turn in her direction. Y'know, Mr. West, there
have been times when I've regretted I was an only child,
but this ain't one of them."

" I fail to see the relevance," began Norman angrily.

" If you're a one only you can't have any nephews or
nieces—law of nature. Tell me something, did you send
Auntie even a proportion of the hundred pounds ? "

" Of course not. The fact is, she has been getting about
a bit more lately, and I fear she has become involved with
people of a better financial standing than herself and she—
well, she finds herself in competition with them. Take this
refugee committee she says she has joined. A number of
rich women making handsome contributions and presumably expecting her to do the same."

" A hundred pounds ? " repeated Crook thoughtfully.
" Quite a sum. Still, couldn't she have settled for less ? "

He nodded his big red head till it seemed as though it
might fall off. " Tell me, when you got her letter—or letters,
I dare say there was more than one—didn't that make you
put your thinking cap on ? "

Violet said, " I told you, Norman—my husband was
going over to Burlham when he could find the time."

" So'm I going to my grave—when I can find the time.
Didn't occur to you someone was putting the pincers on the
old lady ? By the way, did she have any treasure trove,
bangles, geegaws, anything of that sort ? "

" I believe she had a few jewels left her by her mother.
Violet—my wife—did point out to her that if she should
find herself short of funds they constituted a sort of savings
bank . . ."

" If you want a bob or two, stick your ticker up the flue,
go and see your uncle at the three brass balls," hummed
Crook. " Still, I dare say she's run through those before
now. Brandy comes mighty expensive to our pensioners."

" Brandy ? "

" Mean to say you hadn't rumbled ? The whole of Burlham knows it, and don't think any the worse of her. Your
precious law of compensation. That was the first thing little
Miss Grey had on her, could be the only thing. Because
even if the others knew about it who were they to spoil an
old lady's fun ? But Daisy-Bud—ah, she was different.
Passed by the window one evening, doing a bit of snooping
—your blackmailer's a rare snooper—and saw Auntie having
a jam session with a flagon."

" Disgraceful," breathed Violet, who had turned from the
purple to the white variety.

" Be your age," Crook besought her unkindly. " What the
hell is there for a lonely old woman to do these long winter
evenings ? Daren't go out in case she finds someone else's
spoons in her pocket on her return, knows she's only got to
make one slip and she'll find herself incarcerated in something Hitler would have given a month's pay to have thought
of—well, that only leaves a good book and maybe she'd
read all those. No, you take my word for it, the bottle was
her best friend, and little Miss Grey discovered that and
proceeded to cash in."

" A moment ago you said the whole neighbourhood was
aware of the situation," flashed Violet.

" Ho, yes, but none of the others were going to get in
touch with her nevvy."

" She should have told us when this threat was first
voiced," insisted Norman.

" I've known chaps who've got themselves hanged through
sheer carelessness and/or conceit," Crook conceded. " But
I never recall one who sat meekly down and handily wove

his own rope. Why, she'd have sold the roof over her head
sooner than have you know. Desperate situations require
desperate remedies. And, mistakenly or not, people still
believe dead men tell no tales."

They both looked shocked to death. " You can't seriously
mean you are associating my aunt with Miss Grey's murder.
An old woman . . ."

" Knew an old fellow near eighty once. Killed three wives,
all by violence. As you said just now, age ain't just a matter
of years. And it stands to reason someone did it and you
don't go around sticking knives into people's backs because
you've finished your library book and there's nothing good
on the telly. And don't give me the one about it being Mrs.
Cobb, because she's my client so it stands to reason it can't
be her. And one more thing," he added, preparing to
depart to the Whistle and Flute where he'd find company
more to his liking, " if you had any idea about getting the
old lady on the phone and asking awkward questions, let
me, as a lawyer, remind you that withholding information
from the police 'ud make you accessories after the crime, so
it's sometimes smarter to know nothing."

He beamed at them as he plunged for the door.

Poor Miss West! She didn't get much sleep that night
as it was, but she'd have had even less if she realised that
the worst had happened, and Crook had rumbled her, after
all.

CHAPTER XII

THE RUMOUR went round that Crook was back; his yellow car (if that's what you call it, giggled Dacre to Dangerfield) was seen careering majestically through Burlham. But it didn't stop there, it went through to Brightling and parked in the Square. Its owner trudged manfully to The Clover House, where he had a hard-wrung appointment with the proprietrix.

"I'm looking for information," said Crook, "and seeing we both have our livings to get, let's make it snappy. *In re* Miss Marguerite Grey—what can you tell me?"

"Nothing fresh," said Alison in a voice as crisp as one of her own rolls.

"I wonder. Y'see, blackmailers have to start somewhere, and I'm wondering where she began. Would Richard be her first victim, do you suppose?"

The directness of that drove a little colour into Alison's thin distinctive face.

"You're assuming that she was blackmailing him?"

"The whole place knows it," Crook told her gently. "And you told Mrs. Savage that he killed himself because of her and I don't take it he died for love."

"Henrietta appears to have been very accommodating," murmured Alison. "Did she also supply a reason?"

"No. Because she didn't know it. But you know."

"It doesn't affect Hatty," Alison assured him.

"You leave that to Hatty's defence."

"But it's Marguerite's murder, not Richard's death we're discussing now."

"Wouldn't you say the two were linked up? If Richard hadn't died would Marguerite be lyin' in the cold, cold ground?"

"I don't see why not. This—thing—she had learned about Richard, about his past, was very far back, and—you

154

must please believe this, Mr. Crook—if dragging it out would help Hatty I would tell you. But it wouldn't. And it would only hurt those who are still living."

" Meaning self ? " asked the astute Mr. Crook. " Well, who else did he matter to in the sense we mean ? "

" He was like my own son, Mr. Crook."

" There was always the Prodigal of that ilk. Look, why not take your hair down and confide in me ? If it don't help my client I'll be more secret than the grave, which ain't so secret as it used to be, now we're all so blooming clever. What was it she knew about him ? Even if it was something criminal it can't hurt him now."

" There's his memory. One wonders how people stumble on these things, it was so long ago, he was young. I'd moved away, nobody knew anything about us, and he was so full of promise. How could I guess that girl would come like a ghost and—people can commit murder without ever touching the fatal weapon."

" Well, I'm a lawyer," Crook reminded her. " We call it suicide. O.K., you won't break ? Then let's try another approach. How much was Marguerite asking to keep her mouth shut ? "

" All I know is she got a hundred pounds from him, and still no one will admit to giving it to him. He hadn't got it himself, that I do know, he must have got it from someone, I thought it must be Hatty——"

" Break there," said Crook quickly. " What made you pitch on her ? "

" I suppose because I couldn't think of anyone else. He had friends, of course, but no one who would have been likely to supply him with money to that extent. I asked John Savage if he'd made him a loan or advanced his salary, but he said no. I knew I hadn't given it to him—there didn't seem anyone else."

" I thought he was trying to marry her. It don't seem a very propitious beginning."

" She wouldn't have to know why he wanted it. Everyone knows he was extravagant, generous with gifts, he liked the best . . ."

And didn't care who paid for it, Crook reflected, but he prudently kept that to himself.

"Let's have it in the open," said Crook. "Do you think this girl was his mistress and he wanted to pay her off?"

"I'm sure she was nothing of the sort. And she spoke of marriage."

"Only after he couldn't contradict her. Besides, I don't think she would have settled for money, she was all set to become Mrs. Richard Sheridan."

"I'm sure he never intended that. He was after Hatty Savage, but he may have wanted to keep Marguerite quiet until after everything was settled. You remember Hatty saying he proposed a runaway marriage? I've thought so much about that. Once they were man and wife it wouldn't have mattered what Marguerite said."

"So this thing in his past—it didn't imply a prison sentence?"

"Of course not."

"Only, if it had come out, the odds are he'd never have made the grade as John Savage's son-in-law?"

"He obviously thought that," Alison replied carefully. "But in no circumstances would he have married Marguerite. She was quite unsuited to be my nephew's wife. For one thing, there was the disparity in age. He was twenty-one and she was eight-and-twenty. Oh, yes, I found that out after she died. They had to get a birth certificate and there it was in black and white. And all her talk about her father, as if he had been a person of some importance, whereas in fact he was a little tradesman, a small photographer in a place no one had ever heard of; and not even successful at that. Before she came to serve in Bootles the girl was working in some local drapery shop. Of course she got her claws into Richard. I don't believe she had any particular feeling for him, but it meant a lift in the world for her, and she knew about The Clover House, and that it would all come to him in due course."

"Taking a lot for granted, wasn't she?" suggested Crook. "If you hadn't liked the marriage you could have cut him off without even the proverbial shilling."

" Oh, she must have known I wouldn't do that. Richard was all I had, my work was largely for him."

" Oh come," objected Crook, " you and me, we know work's an end in itself. I don't see you sitting on a cushion and sewing a fine seam, not if you had twenty thousand a year."

Alison sighed. " No. That's true. I love my work. I'm rather proud of it. I've built it up from nothing—well, practically nothing. I've seen too many aimless women, who become widows in middle life, or see their children marry and break away and find their days meaningless. I never meant to join that army. But it used to give me pleasure to think I'd have something to leave him, something solid like a wall at his back."

" Coming to the day of the murder," said Crook, who saw no point wasting time or breath when it was obvious it wasn't going to do him any good, " you're sure Miss Grey hadn't told anyone about appearin' as a pore li'l refugee ? "

" I suppose a number of people knew she favoured a tableau with herself as the central figure, but as to her having a dress rehearsal on the day of the luncheon, I for one had no notion she intended to do that. She kept remarkably quiet about it, I'd have warned her that sort of play-acting doesn't go down with people like Lady Martin. She's a horrible woman and the world's snob," she added coolly, " but her very snobbery is an advantage. She's as mean as they come in her own household, always up for the odd halfpenny, but she won't be outdone by any of her inferiors."

" Tell me something. Any remote chance that M.G. had anything on her ? "

" On Lady Martin ? Why, they didn't speak if they met, not unless they were under the same roof. I'm quite sure Marguerite would have been expected to go to the side door if she'd gone calling."

" Well, that was rather the impression I got. Y'know, I'd like to find out where she got her experience. She handled this end quite like the pro. I mean, look how she got her hundred pounds from your nephew, muscled in

here after he'd gone, sent my client out into the wilds tryin'
to raise the ready to shut her mouth——"

" How do people start in a blackmailing career ?   I've
wondered that myself."

" Learn something someone's prepared to pay you for so
long as you keep your mouth shut. Then when you've got
one victim you think, this is a nice simple way of getting a
living and you start looking around for another skeleton.
I've known chaps who've had enough skeletons (other
people's, of course) in their bank accounts to furnish a
churchyard. Still sure you won't tell me what it was started
her off up here ? "

" I beg of you not to try and disinter it," cried Alison.
" It would only make trouble for defenceless people and it
wouldn't get you an inch further in your investigations."

" Nothing to do with the little lad who died in the fire,
I suppose?" offered Crook, drawing a bow at venture like
one more famous than he.

The effect on Miss Sheridan was petrifying ; she was
like someone who has just been warned she is suffering from
an incurable disease and has only a short time to live ; she
looked incredulous and stabbed. It wasn't good grammar
but it was the word that shot into Crook's mind.

" I have heard many infamous things in my time," she
said at last, speaking with difficulty as though her tongue
had suddenly swollen and could no longer be accommodated
by her mouth, " but nothing so shocking as that. To accuse
a dead man . . ."

" I asked a question," Crook pointed out. " Seems I may
have got a bull by chance."

" I didn't realise you knew anything about poor little
Dick. I suppose Henrietta Savage told you."

" If she hadn't I'd have found out."

" Why should you ? "

" Because it's all part of the story, and if you've ever tried
readin' a weekly serial and find one edition's gone west . . ."

" That child died in an accidental fire. Not even you can
suggest that my nephew had anything to do with his death."

" Ever find out who started the fire ? "

" The children were in far too disturbed a state to be questioned. They admitted they had been playing with my lighter and one of them had set the curtains on fire."

" No indication which one ? "

" None. And in any case, even if we knew, that wouldn't be grounds for blackmail. For one thing, there would be no proof, and if there were, a child couldn't be held responsible."

" Those little girls—two, weren't there ?—they didn't say anything to suggest there was more to it than just a silly kid playing with fire ? "

" There was nothing more." Alison spoke with a shocking vehemence.

" And yet you didn't set up a similar establishment elsewhere or re-open on the spot. You took the kid and went into a new neighbourhood, and got yourself another job."

" A thing like that is enough to shake even an iron nerve. If you were a parent yourself—I felt like a mother to all four, particularly to Dickie, who was virtually an orphan. I'd planned to keep him even when the girls left me at the end of the war. It seemed something supremely worth doing, and during the war a lot of us had notions that you, I am afraid, might consider rather highfalutin. And then this tragedy occurred. I felt responsible—well, of course I did. It didn't require anonymous letters or the downright spite of neighbours to make me blame myself. My one desire was to do everything henceforth for the one child no one could take from me. As for the new neighbourhood, have you any conception what an experience like that must have been to a child of five ? Fortunately he was just due to go to school and I found war work in the district. I never pressed him for details, my one hope was that his life wouldn't be warped. And now when he's dead and he can't defend himself you'd try and blacken him in order to whitewash Hatty Cobb. As though Richard wasn't worth a dozen Hatties."

" Live dog better than dead lion," Crook reminded her, looking remarkably unmoved by her outbreak. There'd been some monkey-business about that fire or he was a

Dutchman. And she knew what it was and possibly Marguerite Grey had known as well. That made three of them, including the dead boy. Crook was resolved that before he was much older there'd be four. He wondered how many of the locals would remember a village tragedy nearly twenty years old.

It wasn't difficult to persuade people at Fishers End to talk about Marguerite, the difficulty was to stop them. She had bestowed a kind of vicarious fame upon them by getting herself murdered, and they spoke more kindly of her than they would have done three months before. He easily identified the house where she had lived with her mother, after her father's death, though it was less easy to place the shabby little photographer's where Henry Grey had carried on his unsuccessful business. After his death it had been taken over by a man called Penrose, and although Marguerite had hoped to remain on as assistant—she had been her father's right-hand, they chorused—the new man had a wife who helped in the studio, and Marguerite had had to be satisfied with a job in the local draper's. It was hard to find any particular friend of hers or anyone to whom she had written since her translation to Brightling.

" She always thought herself a cut above the rest of us," said one woman. " None of the local lads were good enough for her, she was going to marry a duke or something. Went away very quietly, no farewells to speak of, and hasn't been back except to visit the cemetery and put a pot plant on her parents' grave." Crook cursed his luck. By rights she should have had a buddy to whom she unburdened herself ; he wondered if she had been resolved to marry Richard Sheridan when she left her home town. She hadn't attempted to get into touch with Alison, everyone was agreed about that, and Richard wasn't much of a catch if he quarrelled with his auntie. Richard's death must have come as a nasty shock, but she hadn't lost heart. Before you could say knife there she was, cosily ensconced in Alison's front parlour, playing the lady, thought Crook, with a simple wonder for the type of mind that could take pleasure in such a footling pursuit.

He went to see the house where the tragedy had occurred, but that didn't exist any more. An enterprising builder had bought it, pulled down what remained and had erected a clutch of little bungalows. Alison had spoken of that house with real affection, a good place for children to grow up, she had said, a garden, space to move, fresh air to breathe. Well, someone else had thought differently. The gardens of the four bungalows were no more than cat runs, the houses themselves were modern, clean, bright and so damned identical that anyone with a breath of individuality would have dropped dead on the threshold. The neighbours had moved out, of course, but he tracked one or two down, he read up the inquest in the local paper, and went to look at the grave in the churchyard. All very discreet, he thought, all very hush-hush. Poor little boy, a terrible thing to happen. And yet he felt convinced there'd been something and Richard had been involved. Only—where precisely did Marguerite come in? Could Alison have known her before the inquest? But no, her hold had been over Richard, it was on his account that she had come to Brightling. There was a dark patch somewhere in his past, and no evidence that it stemmed from that tragic day when the house caught fire.

When he had visited everyone who might be able to help him and consulted every record, he came fleeting back to town, dropped in at Bloomsbury Street and asked Bill if anyone from the Brightling area had been telephoning him. Bill said no.

" Attaboy," murmured Mr. Crook. " I'll be paying them a flying visit myself to-morrow. You know what they do in France, Bill, when they're after a murderer? They reconstruct the crime and make the suspect or suspects line up alongside."

" And you've got a suspect ? "

" You might say I had three. I'll try 'em out during the next forty-eight hours and see which of them breaks."

Down in Brightling and Burlham the situation would have reminded the traveller of those hideous swamps where the mud boils and bubbles, perpetually warning vulnerable humanity of danger close at hand. Hilda West had had a cruel shock when her nephew turned up, without so much as a postcard to herald his arrival, and repeated his threat of having the old woman removed to a suitable nursing home. His aunt, shaken into a new sort of courage, bundled herself into a mantle and bonnet and went to call on Philip Cobb.

"I have come to consult you professionally," she said. "I cannot help feeling that Mr. Crook should have come to see me before calling on my nephew. Has he the right to get me removed to—to an institution against my will?"

"Only if he can get an order," said Philip. "Why, has he threatened to do anything of the sort?"

"He thinks I am quite friendless. I should like to be legally represented in case of an emergency."

"Refer him to me," Philip said, and she went home and wrote to Norman that she had taken advice and had been assured, etc., etc.

When she had posted the letter she went to put it in the box and on the way back she encountered Henrietta.

"Have you any fresh news from Mr. Crook?" she inquired.

"He seems to have vanished."

"He will be back," said Miss West bitterly.

"I hope so. He hasn't been in touch with you?"

"Not yet. In any case, it would be a waste of time. I can tell him nothing. I saw your son-in-law this afternoon," she went on in the same breath. "He's heard nothing either."

Then Lady Martin came sailing out of a side turning, carrying a letter. When she saw the two women talking she said in her graceless staccato way, "I suppose you have both heard from that man also?"

"That man?"

"Crook. I cannot imagine where Philip Cobb found him."

"And he's writing to you?"

" He appears to be under the impression that I can help him in his inquiries. Nonsensical, of course. I have written to tell him so. It would be most inconvenient having him at the house."

" Are you putting him off ? " Henrietta sounded quite awed.

Unexpectedly Miss West began to giggle. " He'll only come down the chimney," she said. " That would be a worse shock."

Lady Martin recalled the gossip that circulated so freely round the village. Disgraceful, she thought, broad daylight and talking to me. She looked hurriedly round as though her snotty-nosed chauffeur might be hiding in a tree or somewhere.

" I think you should go home and lie down—at once," she said. " Have you no relatives you could ask to come and stay ? "

" Why on earth should I want a relative ? It's bad enough when they only come for an hour."

" There's something I wanted to talk to you about," Henrietta improvised. " If I came along at four o'clock . . ."

" Something ought to be done about her," announced Lady Martin, as Miss West moved away. " Everyone knows she drinks like a fish. She's quite irresponsible."

" I've never found her so. What is it Mr. Crook thinks you can tell him ? "

" Perhaps he expects me to name the murderer. It's always a mistake to get mixed up with people like that Miss Grey. It always spells trouble."

" Perhaps he's going the rounds," suggested Henrietta. " I'm sorry if I seem unsympathetic, but then it's my daughter Mr. Crook is trying to get released."

" It must be perfectly obvious that I know nothing, though naturally I should be pleased to help Hatty if I could. As a matter of fact, I think it might be a good thing if I went away for a few days. My husband is a person of some importance, it doesn't help him for my picture to be in the papers."

" What surprises me," Henrietta told her husband that evening, " aren't the murders that do get committed but those that don't. John, do you think he's got anything fresh—Mr. Crook, I mean ? Philip speaks so well of him."

" I saw Arbuthnot to-day," her husband told her. " He's retiring even earlier than he anticipated. This new chap Williams wants to take over at once. It'll mean unseating Philip. It could hardly have come at a worse time."

" I never did like Mr. Arbuthnot, a selfish old man. He and Lady Martin would make a wonderful pair. Anyway, Hatty won't want to stay in Brightling after all this. Didn't Philip speak of going north ? "

" He's speaking now of emigrating."

" Hatty won't like that. She told me she wouldn't agree to going north and of course it does depend on her to some extent."

" If things don't go as we hope," said John heavily, " steps will have to be taken to release the funds. You know, Henry, I wonder how he bears up at all. It's bad enough for us. And now he's virtually being put out of practice here. I call it infamous of Arbuthnot truckling to public opinion like this. By the way, d'you know when Crook will be back ? "

" He's written to Lady Martin. For all I know he's written to all the other committee members—not Miss West, though. Unless her letter's in the post."

She rang up Alison to know if she had heard, but there was nothing in her mail either.

So they settled down to wait.

They didn't have to wait long. Crook came down the following day and fulfilled his promise to call at Grandison House.

" I'm proposing a small experiment," he said. " Be glad of your co-operation. If you agree," he added sycophanti- cally, before she could refuse, " the others 'ull string along. It's always useful to have a spare arrow in your quiver when you're visiting among strangers."

" What is the nature of the experiment ? "

" I want to get the committee round to Miss Sheridan's house and go through what happened that day."

" We don't know what happened that day."

" That's why."

" What do the others say ? "

" I haven't asked 'em yet. I thought I'd start at the top. Like I said, if I tell them you're coming they'll catch on all right. And if any of them don't," he added coolly, " that'll be the time to start doin' a bit of arithmetic."

Mrs. Waltham said she didn't see how she could help, but if Lady Martin had agreed, he, Crook, could count on her. There was no need to hold out any bait to Dacre or Dangerfield, they'd have given a subscription to any fund he liked to name to be in at the death, as they'd ghoulishly have put it. Henrietta said, " Are you really on to something ? " and he said, " Desperate situations require desperate measures. I don't say it's going to be pleasant for everyone, but then it ain't very pleasant for my client whiling away her time in gaol."

He asked Philip Cobb if he would stand in for Hatty. " I want the right number of people," he explained. " I've been on to Miss Sheridan ; she's going to act for the corpse."

Cobb said, " I don't know what you're up to, Crook, but take care you don't end up with another body before you're through."

But Crook said callously he knew his onions and anyway they didn't hang for knifing any more, simply inviting murderers to do their stuff, if you asked him.

And off he went to acquaint Miss West with his plan.

" But why do you want me ? " the poor old biddy implored him.

Crook sent her a brilliant glance from his bright brown eyes.

" Because, believe it or not, you're goin' to be my star witness."

But later he telephoned to Henrietta to ask if she could collect the old lady and bring her along.

" She trusts me about as much as I trust the Chancellor

of the Exchequer," he said. "And I've got to have her there. Don't start sympathising with anyone, sugar, except your daughter. The rest can sink or swim, but by hook or crook we've got to bring her ashore and this is the only way I can think of to do it."

CHAPTER XIII

" I SHALL SAY it again, and as often as I please. It's a wicked waste of good food."

Lady Martin glared at the company assembled in Alison's sitting-room. That one, Crook reflected, wouldn't need a knife. Lightning flashed from her eyes and he noticed with interest that for all her claims to noble birth she had what he called butcher's hands.

They were all collected round a table spread more or less as it had been on the day of Marguerite's murder. Crook had gone patiently from one committee member to another asking his questions and making notes of the replies he received. Now he fished a bit of paper out of his pocket and read : Aspics, patties, canapés (whatever they may be when they're at home), sausage rolls, bridge rolls, sandwiches, tipsy cake—is that what they call trifle nowadays ?—gâteaux. Have I forgotten anything ? They told him fish salad, so he added that to his list. Mrs. Dacre took some comfort from the fact that forks and spoons had been provided, so perhaps when the ordeal was over they'd be allowed to tuck in.

The dividing curtain had been pulled back and the canvas and the ceramics and all the heterogeneous spoils the ardent Marguerite had amassed were on show as they had been on that fatal day. Philip Cobb stood, paper-white, by the window. Henrietta was watching Miss West, more tense than ever. Lady Martin looked scornful, Mrs. Waltham apprehensive ; Dacre and Dangerfield were as eager as jackals on the prowl.

" What is the notion of this ? " Lady Martin snapped. " It appears to me most theatrical."

" Well, I'll want a witness, won't I ? " urged Crook. " I ain't a policeman, and if I were I'd have brought a sergeant along. Even a plumber," he besought winningly, " is allowed his mate."

Mrs. Waltham gave a decorous little crow of laughter, but that dried when she realised that her ladyship was not amused.

" What are we waiting for ? " she inquired.

" The lady of the house. Ah, here she comes."

Alison entered, haggard but distinguished by an unquenchable elegance. She sat down in the chair Marguerite had occupied.

" Is this where you want me ? "

" If you don't mind. The rest can dispose themselves as they please."

Philip Cobb spoke. " Are you hoping one of the company will betray herself ? " he asked.

" In murder," Crook told him, " it's as much How ? as Who ? "

That startled them all. " You mean, you *know* ? "

" I'm paid to know," said Crook. " Now—we've whittled the time factor pretty fine. We've got the last person who admits to seeing her alive—that's Miss Sheridan—and the first person we know for certain saw her dead."

" That would be the murderer," objected Cobb.

" That's what I said. Now, Miss West, we start with you, seeing you were the first on the scene."

" No," interrupted Henrietta, " Miss West and I came in together."

" That was the second time. I'm referrin' to the time Miss West came up here alone. What made you do it ? " he added, his brown eyes about as soft as bits of stone.

" No," whispered the old woman. " It wasn't I ! I swear it wasn't. She was dead already. I promise you, Mr. Crook, she was dead already."

If Crook had been looking for a sensation he had it on his hands now.

" What makes you think Miss West came up earlier ? "
Henrietta demanded.

" Why, you told me so yourself, sugar. You and Miss
West were having a little chat about bazaars and she said
how things had changed, it always used to be tray-mats and
home-made jam and now it was surrealism and—what's the
word ?—ceramics. Well, how did she know about that
picture bein' there if she hadn't peeked behind the curtain ?
And don't give me the one about Marguerite telling her,
because I've had a word with Miss Sheridan here and she
says it hadn't arrived the night before. Must have come
along that morning . . ."

" Oh, it did," said Alison. " Marguerite showed it to
me."

" And if anyone doubts that, I've got evidence. Well,
then, how did you know it was there, Miss West ? "

All life seemed to have died out of the old woman's face.

" I knew it was too good to be true that you wouldn't
find out. But I didn't kill her, Mr. Crook. She was dead
when I drew the curtain back."

" What made you do that ? "

" I came round a little early. I had to see her. She was
threatening me, through my nephew. He didn't know
about my—my weakness, and he had warned me that if I
caused him any more embarrassment he would get me
committed to a—a home or something. He said I wasn't
responsible."

" And she was threatenin' to write to him ? "

" I told her it would be a waste of time. Norman wouldn't
have given her the money."

" How much money ? "

" She was asking a hundred pounds. I thought perhaps
I could raise it on my diamond ring, but it wasn't so good as
I thought or else diamonds have lost their value. The best
offer I got was sixty pounds. I went round to ask her if she
would accept that."

" Taking the money ? "

" I hadn't actually sold the ring ; there was no sense
doing so if she insisted on her—her pound of flesh. Besides,"

anger flashed suddenly in the faded eyes that must once have been so fine, " it had been my mother's ring, I didn't see why she should have it. We had managed to cling to that through all our vicissitudes—I didn't see why she should have it," she repeated.

" Who let you in ? " Crook was severely practical.

" The door was on the latch and the card in place. I had never been inside the house before, but I came into the hall, expecting she would hear me and call out. But no one did, so I came up here. The table was spread and the curtain was drawn. I thought perhaps she hadn't quite finished dressing. I came back to the landing. It was a very strange feeling, to find myself in a house that wasn't mine, I felt like a burglar. I listened but there wasn't a sound. There's something, a kind of sixth sense perhaps, that warns you when you're in an empty house and I got that feeling then. But when it was twenty minutes to one I began to think she must be here, she was playing with me, cat and mouse, watching me from somewhere, laughing perhaps. She liked a sense of power, there are others who could tell you that."

" So you pulled back the curtain ? "

" Yes. For a second I only saw that terrible picture, then I saw her in the chair beyond where Miss Sheridan is sitting now, sort of bowed over it . . ."

" And she didn't move ? "

" No. I even wondered if she could have dropped off . . ."

" And your eye fell on the knife on the table, and you grabbed it up—come, sugar, let's have a few facts. It was what they call an uncontrollable impulse. Hard to blame you at that. I dare say she'd got you to the pitch where you were afraid to answer the telephone and left letters unopened all day . . ."

" No, no," cried the old woman, " it wasn't like that at all. At first, you must believe me, I didn't realise what had happened. I—I began to laugh. 'What a joke,' I said. 'How long were you going to wait ? Or was it a trap ? Did you think I'd try and steal—steal . . .'"

" Steal what ? " asked Crook, who seemed less moved than any of them.

" Anything," she whispered, " just food, perhaps."

Henrietta watched him with a look that was almost hate ; Philip Cobb's face expressed disgust. The others were all shamelessly intent, even Lady Martin had temporarily forgotten her blue blood. They all had a horrific vision of the old woman standing beside a dead body, laughing, taunting.

" Isn't it macabre ? " Dacre's hand came stealing out to clutch her friend's. This was the real stuff.

" I said, ' Joke's over,' and when she didn't move I put out my hand and caught her shoulder, and the little black shawl slipped, and I saw the knife. Mr. Crook, I thought I would die."

He'd heard the phrase often enough ; in his room at the top of the tall building in Bloomsbury Street men and women of every age and social category had stared into his face and said it or its equivalent, and he had always replied, " Well, that's what I'm here for, ain't it ? To see you don't." But he didn't say that now.

" There was a telephone on the premises," he pointed out. " Why not get the police ? "

" The police could have done nothing for her. I realised that. And how could I prove I hadn't had a hand in it myself ? "

" Well, I don't know about that, of course. But it was your one hope. If you could have shown you'd only just arrived and the body was chilling . . ."

" It didn't occur to me, I just wanted to get away. I knew the others would be there soon, let them find her, I thought. I went down the stairs and I looked up and down the road. I didn't think anyone else would be coming just yet, but when I reached the gate I saw Mrs. Savage turning the corner from Anson Street. She was bound to see me if I came into the road, so I went back to the step and pressed the bell and waited for her."

" And when she came you didn't think of saying, ' A shocking thing's happened. Someone's stabbed Miss Grey ' ? "

" How could I. I should have laid myself open to the worst kind of misconstruction ? I should have had to admit, under police questioning, that I was in her power, that she was threatening me . . ."

" Anything in writing ? "

" No. No. She would ring up and whisper just as she did that day. 'You know who this is . . .' or sometimes just, 'I thought I'd have a word with you. Have you been thinking of what we discussed last time we met ? ' "

" So there wasn't anything, bar what you chose to tell them, to put you under suspicion ? "

" You are a lawyer, Mr. Crook. You must know the police."

" And not the only one, it seems. About this telephone call now. Couldn't have dreamt it or anything ? "

" Of course not. Both Hatty and myself received calls from Miss Grey . . ."

" So you've both told me. Funny thing, the telephone people can't trace any calls made from this number the day the lady died."

Philip Cobb stirred. " I can assure you, my wife received a call summoning her here for half past twelve."

" I don't say she didn't. I only say it wasn't made from this number. Of course, Miss Grey might have gone to the box over the green, only why should she ? And then she'd be dolled up like a refugee. Make any calls yourself that day, Miss West ? "

" I—really I don't remember."

" Oh come, you don't do yourself justice. Your neighbours don't get murdered every day of the week. You'd recall every detail."

" I may have made a call or two—tradesmen, perhaps."

" Liquor shop ? Well, we could track that. If you can give me the number."

She shook her head wildly. " I may have had three or four local calls. But I can promise you I didn't ring Mrs. Cobb. If I'd asked her to come at half past twelve I wouldn't be here myself at twenty minutes to one."

" Oh, you can corroborate the time ? I hadn't got

that." Crook sounded as courteous as the Cheshire Cat.

" Mrs. Savage knows I was on the doorstep . . ."

" She don't know how long you'd been there, though, or how long you'd been upstairs first. Y'see, the idea—speaking as defence lawyer, you understand—'ud be for Mrs. Cobb, a likely suspect if ever there was one—to find herself alone with the corpse. Got an alibi for twelve-twenty, say ? "

Miss West shook her head.

" That's the trouble in this case. Statements, statements, everywhere, and not a scrap of proof."

Henrietta leaned forward. " Mr. Crook, do you seriously believe Miss West killed Marguerite ? "

" I'd suspect a hippopotamus if it happened to be on the scene at the right time," replied Crook readily, " but no, in point of fact I don't think she did. You're her alibi."

They all looked pardonably startled at that. Crook enlightened them.

" Y'see, you more or less told me she'd been in the room before any of the rest of you, and it was possible she'd made the calls, but you also said she'd come without gloves. Well, if she wasn't wearing gloves there'd be finger-prints on the knife."

" But I thought everyone knew you wiped them off," exclaimed Mrs. Dacre before she could stop herself.

" I can see I'm going to have a dandy time when you're being arraigned for a bit of corpse-dealing," Crook congratulated her. " But a chap who remembers that also remembers to wipe his finger-prints off everything else, and there were her prints all over the room. Door handle, bell, window-frame—a guilty person would have been careful to leave no prints anywhere."

" Wouldn't that be suspicious ? " asked Alison, speaking for the first time. " We all knew Miss West had been here."

" Amateurs always try and play safe, too safe," Crook told her. " Of course it 'ud be more natural to have a few prints found along of all the rest, but murderers are more single-minded than most. They're the centre of their universe and that gives them the idea they're the centre of everyone else's too. Ninety-nine times out of a hundred no one's paying them any attention at all, but you'll never get them to believe that. The hundredth case is the chap who gets away. Well, that lets Miss West out. I can't for the life of me see why Lady Martin or Mrs. Waltham should take a chance, and anyway their alibis are as firm as Gibraltar Rock. Mrs. Dacre and her friend came late and they have alibis too. And though I'm like the White Queen, who could believe six impossible things before breakfast, I can't believe that Mrs. Savage would let her daughter lie in gaol when she could winkle her out at a word."

They all looked at him, beyond speech now.

" Ever read *Alice Through the Looking-Glass* ? " he inquired conversationally.

" What on earth has Alice got to do with it ? " demanded Lady Martin in irritable tones.

" You remember whenever she approached something she found she was walking in the opposite direction, but when she turned her back she got there at once ? Well, it seemed to me that could apply here. We've been saying, who wanted to murder Marguerite Grey ? But suppose the point at issue was—who wanted Hatty Cobb out of the way ? Whoever it was would never get a better opportunity. Who would profit by Daisy-Bud's death ? Hatty Cobb. Who was known to have had a call to come early ? Hatty Cobb."

" But Marguerite had sent the message," said Mrs. Waltham stupidly.

Dacre and Dangerfield joined in excitedly to tell her no, she hadn't, that had obviously been the murderer.

Crook beamed at them. " Give it a name," he urged.

Dacre wilted but Dangerfield returned, " That's what you're going to do, I hope."

"Y'see, if people see something that looks like a lion they think it is a lion, and if someone rings up and says I'm Marguerite Grey, then it don't seem to occur to them it ain't Marguerite Grey. But, of course, it don't follow. I might ring you," he turned to the frozen Lady Martin, " and say I'm the P.M. and would your husband be pre-

pared to consider takin' over my job, but that wouldn't
prove I was the Prime Minister, would it ? "

Henrietta spoke—a low incredulous voice in that hum of
speculation.

" But who would hate Hatty so ? " she asked.

" It's a mistake to think hate's always behind violent
crime, half the time it's just expediency. Chaps who knock
down or strangle a night watchman haven't got anything
special against him, except that he's in the way. Too bad
for him, but you treat him as you'd treat a rock that blocked
your road when you were out drivin'. They don't start
feeling about 'em till things go wrong and there's a chance of
them being brought to book. Now—who benefits if my
client's tucked away for a number of years ? " He looked
at them expectantly. " We've franked Miss West, we know
Miss Sheridan was in Brightling and even if she'd had
murder in mind she couldn't have got back between twelve,
when she has an alibi, and the time the body was found—
not even if she was drivin' the Scourge. Which seems to
leave the husband." He turned like lightning on Philip
Cobb, who just stared. " Care to tell us where you were at,
say, twelve o'clock ? "

" In my office, of course. If you want an alibi . . ."

" No, I believe you. Made a few telephone calls round
about that time, didn't you ? "

" I dare say. I often do."

" Local calls, I wouldn't wonder."

" Most probably."

" And twelve-fifteen ? Where were you then ? "

" On my way to Askham to lunch with a client."

Crook's red brows jumped like a skipping ram. " Seem
to remember your mentioning lunch was one o'clock."

" That's right."

" Not walking, by any chance ? "

" Naturally not."

" Oh, I get it. Bike. I'm told they're coming back ;
more manœuvrable in traffic."

" Car," said Philip equably.

" You must let me take you out one of these days, give

you a wrinkle or two. I mean, forty-five minutes to go—
how many miles ? "

" About sixteen. I stopped *en route* to telephone my wife
but she was out."

" Why ring from a call-box ? "

" Because I was on the road."

" Oh, I see. Didn't think of ringing before you left the
office."

" That's right."

" Still, you were allowing rather more time than you
wanted, weren't you ? Or did it hang heavy on your
hands ? "

" My watch was fast. I didn't realise it till I reached the
post office at the cross-roads."

" Well, that's a new one anyway," commented Crook.
" Usually the watch was slow. What time did you make
Askham ? "

" I suppose about a quarter to one."

" And you dropped into the Goat and Compasses for a
quick one, and unfortunately you didn't see anyone you
knew ? "

" As a matter of fact, I browsed round a second-hand
bookshop for a quarter of an hour."

" Buy anything ? "

" Nothing caught my fancy."

" So what it amounts to is you left your office soon after
twelve o'clock, having made at least two local calls, and
can't produce anyone to support your alibi until 1 p.m.,
when you fossicked up to the Colonel's table."

Nothing seemed able to shake Philip's calm. " It didn't
occur to me I should require an alibi."

Miss West could endure it no longer. " But, Mr. Crook,
it was Mr. Cobb who called you in."

" Ever read a book called *At the Villa Rose* ? " Crook
wondered. " Oh, it was a honey. Young chap in that,
worships the ground his girl treads on, she gets held for the
murder of a rich old trout, he goes haring off to pull in
France's most famous detective, and come to that, the most
likeable detective of all time, bar none. No one but you

can clear the girl I love, he says. You'd have fallen for him right flat on your face, sugar. So—in comes M. Hanaud, and there's our hero signing his death-warrant on the dotted line."

" But Mr. Cobb is her husband," insisted Hilda West.

" Any rozzer could tell you when a married pair comes to grief their first suspect is the survivor. Clear him (or her) first, and then start getting out after the next in line."

" Then—are you saying it was Mr. Cobb who telephoned, pretending to be Marguerite ? Oh, but he couldn't. He's my lawyer."

" Give him a chance," urged Philip, " and he'll explain how I managed to sound like Miss Grey on the telephone and then what advantage it is to me to have my wife found guilty."

" Well, she ain't going to be," Crook assured him promptly. " As for point one "—he dropped his voice. " Is that you, dear ? " he asked in a mysterious whisper. " You won't forget you're expected to lunch, will you ? Something like that ? "

" Yes. Yes, that's how it was."

" And if you'd had your eyes shut, could you have sworn it wasn't Marguerite Grey speaking ? "

" I don't believe I could. Though I wouldn't have known precisely who it was."

" So I go round, stick a knife between the lady's shoulders, find the incriminating letters and put them in the stove— why don't I take them away with me ? "

" Well, there had to be some proof that your lady wife had been on the premises. If the letters weren't there— someone else might have removed them, you think ? Just tell me who."

Philip Cobb looked like a man engrossed in a chess problem of such complexity that he had thought for no one else ; he didn't even seem to appreciate the situation Crook was building up around him.

" I leave my office a little after twelve. I reach the cottage, I dispose of Miss Grey, I discover and destroy the letters—having previously arranged with my wife to be on the spot at half past twelve. Pretty tricky, wasn't it ? I mean, we might have met on the doorstep."

" Only as it happens she didn't get there till twelve-fifty."

" And I had second sight and knew the car was going to break down."

" You wouldn't need second sight to know that."

" Oh come," Philip protested, " did I tamper with the car as well ? Why not see to it that it's wrecked altogether ? "

" Because we need a victim, of course. Someone had to murder Marguerite Grey in order to put Hatty Cobb on the spot."

" You still haven't explained my advantage . . ."

" Oh, didn't I ? Well, it's common knowledge you've set your heart on this practice in the north and Mrs. C. didn't see it your way. You can't go ahead without she gives you the say-so, and that she ain't prepared to do. You don't want to hang around playing second fiddle to a new-comer —you didn't marry a rich man's daughter for that. But—if she's found guilty of murder and gets a life sentence you could look to your father-in-law to ease conditions. In the circumstances you couldn't go too far north for him."

Philip Cobb had caught hold of the back of a chair and stood flexing his fingers round the curved wood. He said abruptly to Henrietta, " You don't believe a word this chap says, do you ? You know I didn't marry Hatty for her money. And of course I wasn't near the house on the day Marguerite Grey died."

" In another minute," suggested Crook admiringly, " you'll be telling us who was."

" I think I could tell you." It was Miss West's courteous old voice, and if the carpet had jumped up and bitten him Crook couldn't have looked more startled.

" I thought you didn't arrive till after the lady was dead. If you've been double-crossing me . . ."

" A quite fantastic suggestion," said Miss West, " and I can't tell you her identity, but . . ."

" Her ? "

" Oh, yes, I think it would have to be a woman. And, of course, I can't prove that she murdered Miss Grey, but she must have come here, and it would be rather too much of a coincidence for two people to have come in that brief time."

" Don't shoot till you see the whites of their eyes," advised Crook. " What makes you so certain it was a lady ? "

" Well, Miss Sheridan really. She said that when she went at half past eleven Miss Grey was setting the table and she was still wearing an overall. But when I arrived and found her she was in that black dress. Now do you see ? "

" No," said Crook stolidly.

" She couldn't have fastened herself into that. It has about forty minute fastenings up the back, and the bodice fits like a skin, and was boned too. Bodices were always boned at the beginning of the century. No one, Mr. Crook, not even a snake could have achieved it."

" But she's right," cried Henrietta. " We remarked at the time that that dress must have been made in the days of ladies' maids."

" Yes. Zippers only came in when ladies' maids went out."

" If it had occurred to you, Crook, that I might have been pressed into the job," said Philip softly, " I had a bandaged finger that week, caught it in the door of the car and it was splinted. I could hardly do up my own buttons, let alone about forty hooks and eyes. And that at least is something that can be proved."

" I knew if we got together we'd winkle out the truth," said Crook coolly. " The Day of Judgment," thought Henrietta, " would probably find him unmoved."

" So we are back where we started," Alison suggested crisply. " The only people who might have come early were Miss West and—Hatty Cobb. Either of them, I suppose, could have dealt with those fastenings . . ."

" Not I," said Miss West firmly. " They need far better sight than I have possessed for years."

" Then—I'm sorry, Mr. Crook, but what other choice have you ? We know Hatty was expected here at twelve-thirty . . ."

" Expected by whom ? Remember, Marguerite didn't

make the calls. I'll tell you. Expected by the one who did phone, havin' previously set the scene. And if you was to lift up your eyes and look right ahead, my guess is you'd see her."

Startled, Alison looked up to behold a white, drawn face and eyes bright with fever, staring her down from the gilt-edged looking-glass on the opposite wall.

"You can't mean—you're mad. Of course you are. I was at Brightling at twelve o'clock, and I can prove it."

"That's not the proof I'm lookin' for," said Crook. "Can you prove that Marguerite Grey was alive *when you left the house* ?"

"The medical evidence," Alison began, but Crook shook his big bullet head.

"The doctor was told there was evidence that the girl was alive at midday, so he put time of death as near to twelve o'clock as possible. Tell him your proof's gone up like smoke and he'll agree death could have taken place, say, half an hour earlier."

"Proof ? " murmured Mrs. Waltham, who was fascinated but dazed by this development.

"Well, we know Miss Grey didn't make the calls, because there's no record."

"The telephone authorities are very lax," insisted Alison. "Why, only the other day in the House of Commons the Postmaster-General admitted there was frequent confusion about charges."

"I seem to remember that was trunk calls, and they were over-charges. You show me any telephone authority that charges too little and I'll eat my hat for breakfast." He looked at it lovingly, a hideous hard brown felt as bright as a horse-chestnut.

"My difficulty is the same as Mr. Cobb's," said Alison, apparently unmoved by his confidence. "Why should I take this immense risk ? "

"Because the only safe blackmailer is the dead black-mailer. It's like a cancer, if you don't get it cut out in time it kills you. And you didn't fancy having little Miss Grey eating you up year after year . . ."

" And, of course, you have proof that that was the case ? "

Crook nodded. " I'm a lawyer, I don't speak without the book. Got something to show you," he added confidingly to the party, taking a big shabby wallet from his pocket. From among a welter of papers he produced a photograph that he laid on Henrietta's knee. " Ring a bell ? " he suggested.

The picture showed a small handsome child with a smooth dark poll, grasping a toy and staring impudently into the eye of the camera.

" It's Richard Sheridan," agreed Henrietta, handing it on to Miss West. " What a charming study. I don't think I ever saw that one before."

Miss West bent her old face close to the photograph. " Dear me ! " she said with a sigh, " it seems so sad that his father could never have seen him at that age."

She looked round vaguely and handed it on to Philip Cobb.

" Oh well," said Crook cosily, " I don't suppose it would have meant a thing to him. That ain't a picture of Richard Sheridan, that's little Dickie Smith. Sheridan's been in Leffingham churchyard these fifteen years and more. That's what Marguerite Grey knew, and that's why she had to die."

The silence that followed was broken by Alison. She was laughing and the sound froze their marrows, as Dacre confided to Dangerfield when this most fascinating of gatherings finally broke up.

" Really, Mr. Crook, what will you think of next ? Not that that isn't a very ingenious theory, only I'm afraid not susceptible of proof."

" That's what you think," said Crook. " Maybe you'd care to explain how the original, the negative don't they call it, of this picture is filed in the late Mr. Grey's storehouse labelled D. Smith and your then address."

" Oh, he was a dreadful old muddler," said Alison easily. " I wasn't the least surprised to hear his business was on the rocks. He simply confused the two boys."

" Oh ! " said Crook. " So you took them both in to be done ? "

" If you'd ever looked after children you'd know one of the worst things you have to contend with is jealousy. If I'd had my nephew photographed and left Dickie at home . . ."

" How about the girls ? "

" There was no need to have them done. One of them had a family of her own to whom she would eventually be re-united, the other, like Dickie, had no one."

" If he had no one, why have Dickie photographed ? "

" As I explained to you, Henrietta," casually she by-passed Mr. Crook, "I hoped to get his mother interested in him."

" I remember."

" So what happened to that negative ? " inquired Crook.

Alison shrugged. " I suppose the old man realised we shouldn't be wanting any more prints and he destroyed it."

" And at the same time he destroyed the record of Richard Sheridan ? "

" I suppose so."

" And does that explain how it was that Marguerite recognised Dickie Smith in the churchyard ? Because she did, you know."

" I thought you'd never met Marguerite," snapped Alison.

" I've still got something that works for me here." Crook tapped his big bumpy forehead. " It was after that meeting that everything started to change. Mrs. Cobb noticed it, other people round about noticed it. Can't blame the boy exactly. Must have been a shock when he'd been brought up to think of himself as springing from sound stock to find his mum was no better than she should be and he can take his choice from dads all the way from the muckraker to the milkman."

" May I be permitted to see that photograph ? " asked Alison. And he gave it her readily.

" I've got a duplicate if you should take a fancy to that one," he warned her.

CHAPTER XIV

" FUNNY THING," observed Crook to the party at large,
" she put the weapon into my hands herself. She told me
Daisy-Bud's dad was a photographer, and she used to
help him. Well, if she hadn't ever made use of his services
how would she know about him at all ? So I went along
just to have a look-see. No trace of a Richard Sheridan,
they said, but there was a record that a Miss Sheridan had
brought in a boy called Dickie Smith—same first name
really, which must have been a help—and they obligingly
rootled out a print for me."

" You hadn't seen the boy, had you ? " Philip asked.

" Didn't matter. I got hold of a recent photo of him."
He whipped that out of an envelope and showed it to them
and Henrietta recognised that at once. There was a fac-
simile of it on Alison's dressing-table. " I took a bit of professional advice and I'm assured the two pictures are of the
same lad, barring he had a twin brother, of course, which
we know he didn't. So doing a bit of arithmetic—she played
it very neat." It struck Henrietta with a sort of horror that
they were talking of Alison as though she weren't there.
" Took the boy into a new neighbourhood, .saw to it he
didn't come into contact with the two girls, who might have
blown the gaff, even had the inquest in a strange town, and
I dare say even the dead boy's mum might have had some
difficulty in recognising her son—and to a stranger one
small boy is remarkably like another, and why should anyone
think she'd give the wrong identification ? "

" Why did she ? " Lady Martin's harsh voice disturbed
the tense air.

" There was a will," explained Crook, " and a damn' bad
will at that. If it had been me I wouldn't have drawn it up.
Under that will she came into her brother's fortune such as
it was, provided she made a home for his son till he was

sixteen. She got the income till then and after that the capital. Dad seems to have been on the austere side and thought the boy could look after himself thereafter ; and of course by then he should have muscled in on Auntie's industry. I've seen the will," he added, " and there's no let-up if anything goes wrong, the boy dies or proves unmanageable. In that case, the whole caboodle goes to Henry Sheridan's old college. Well, here's her problem. Through no fault of her own, the boy's dead, and her future's pretty bleak. Back to the school-teaching she hated, same old grind till the day she becomes eligible for the retirement pension, all her dreams gone whistling down the wind. And after all who was she cheating except a mouldy old institution that 'ud manage to raise the funds from some other quarter." He looked up and met Philip Cobb's shocked gaze. " Oh, yes, brother," he assured him, " that's the way their minds work. So—take a chance, identify the wrong boy, switch the ration books, I dare say they wore the same pants and jerseys ; there's no heart-broken parents to cope with and, to cap it all, the lady-help falls under a lorry or something ; she's the only one who might have blown the gaff. Why, the situation was hand-tailored for madam here. She couldn't have foreseen Marguerite Grey."

He had a theory that crime's never a hundred per cent safe because of the invisible witness, the woman walking her dog or the man quarrelling with his wife and barging out of the house at 2 a.m. and so seeing something he wasn't meant to see. Alison, he admitted, had played it very neatly. And then out of the past, like some melodrama of the Victorian era, came the round, smiling, dumpy figure of Marguerite Grey.

" She must have recognised him in the churchyard, and blown the gaff before she knew what she was doing," Crook went on. " Can't you picture it ? Handsome young man looking helplessly around for a grave he's never seen before, and the way the population of cemeteries increases is a shock to us all. Little pussy sees him and pops over. ' Can I help you ? ' (Or he could have seen her, I suppose, and asked if she could help him, but my guess is it was the other way

round.) " He went into an act that left them all gasping.
" ' Why, surely, excuse me, I don't mean to intrude, but
surely it's Dickie Smith ? ' ' Oh, come, angel, you can do
better than that. Dickie Smith indeed ! I'm the unac-
knowledged heir of all the Russias.' ' But I remember you
perfectly well, really I do. You haven't changed a bit, just
grown up. You came to the studio when you were only so
high, with Miss Sheridan . . .' ' Hey, sugar, how come you
have my name so pat ? ' ' Well, but we all remember her,
though I wasn't very old myself at the time.' (Eye-balls
going like marbles, see ?) ' The fire and the little boy
suffocated or something. We didn't know it was her own
nephew, though, we thought it was the other one, and she
went away directly afterwards. Did she sort of adopt you
in his place ? ' ' Well, the greatest of these, sugar, is charity
and you could put it that way. Want to know a secret ? I'm
passing myself off as Richard Sheridan these days.' Marguerite's as earnest as they come, no more sense of humour
than a silver spoon, and that can't have much or it wouldn't
let itself get pushed around the way it does from one aristocratic mouth to the next. ' But that isn't right, unless, of
course, you've changed your name by deed poll.' Oh, it
was a stroke of pure gold to her, and the worst possible luck
for you, Miss Sheridan, that of all the people who might
have been tending their graves that day he should have to
run up against that female tarantula, but that's the way it
goes, only you can never make criminals see it."

" I don't call it so very criminal," said Mrs. Dacre boldly.
" She wasn't really robbing anyone of the money—you can't
count a silly old college—and she was giving a name and a
background to someone who had neither. And she regarded
him as her son."

" Maybe," agreed Crook grimly, " but that didn't stop
her putting out his light when it became convenient."

That was a shock for which none of them appeared
prepared.

" You're seriously suggesting that I was responsible for
my nephew's death." Alison's voice shook with scorn.

" Well——" Crook hesitated. " O.K. Let it ride. Simpler

to go on referring to him as your nephew maybe, so long as we all remember who we're talking about. And, just as a makeweight, I've got another witness, the plain girl who was taken back by her family, and who's married now and still lives in the same street where she was born. If need be she'll come into court and swear to the identity of the photograph. Still, I don't think the rest of us need much more confirmation. About Richard—he never gave me the notion he was the type of chap who'd meekly put his head in a gas oven because a girl had turned him down. Mind you, I dare say it would have suited his book very nicely to be John Savage's son-in-law, but he'd got Auntie where he wanted her—remember?" He stretched out his big arm and doubled up his formidable fist. "That's what he said. 'I've got her like that.' And everyone supposed he meant Hatty Cobb but my guess 'ud be it was Miss Sheridan he had in mind. And, of course, that 'ud explain his proposal of a runaway marriage; once the knot was tied it wouldn't matter so much if the truth came out, they'd be man and wife and—well, it might be a mite awkward for your daughter to come back and be a girl again. Folk are inclined to whisper behind their hands, ain't they, about unofficial honeymoons." He caught sight of Philip Cobb's face, and hurried on. "Trouble is with all criminals they only see one step ahead. Put Richard out and the secret's safe, The Clover House is safe. But how about little Daisy-Bud waitin' in the wings?"

Henrietta said, "But Alison didn't see Richard that night, she was in bed."

"Who says? I don't think so, I think she was waiting up to hear the result of Richard's proposal to Hatty Savage."

"There's no proof he ever made any such proposal," said Alison scornfully. "And I could have warned him it was a waste of breath if he had. Besides, he hadn't expected to get the opportunity. Hatty was over the moon for Alan Duke, everyone knew it."

"And yet she spent a lot of time that evening with Richard Sheridan."

"Only because Duke stood her up at the eleventh hour,

and very unpleasant she was about it, according to Richard. Quite hysterical, and then she bamboozled herself into the idea that Richard had proposed a runaway match. Well, she had to salvage her pride somehow. She couldn't be let down."

Stood up—let down. Henrietta shook her head. What absurd expressions everyone used nowadays.

" Now, come," said Crook severely, " we've had speculation enough for one day."

" Look who's talking ! " Alison laughed again and a current of cold air seemed to flow through the room. " And this doesn't happen to be speculation."

" You mean, he told you she was hysterical and proved it by producing the sleeping-tablets ? It could be he was afraid she might do herself a mischief," he added thoughtfully, " and that's why he took them. When did he tell you all this, by the way ? Well," as she stared at him, flabbergasted at last, momentarily beyond speech, rubbing her sweating cheeks and forehead with her handkerchief, " it's a simple question, ain't it ? When did he tell you that Duke had stood the girl up and that's why she had time to bring him home ? When he got in ? " He shook his big head. " How come ? You were in bed, you said so. So—next day ? Only next morning he was in bed and he never woke up. I'm not a bad hand at solving a mystery myself, but this one has me beat."

Alison leaned back, she appeared to have recovered from that moment of instantaneous shock.

" Of course," she said. " All this rubbish about faked photographs and so forth has got me confused. It wasn't that night he told me about Duke, but the night before."

" The night before Hatty was at home with us, we had people to dinner," said Henrietta dully.

" And the night before that 'ud be a Sunday. No, you planned it very neat, but you forgot one thing. The phial. I suppose when he came in and told you Hatty had advised him to go to the devil in this way, and flourished the tablets, you said—what would she say ? " He appealed to Henrietta.

" Give me those at once," said Henrietta mechanically.

" And seeing he never meant to use them, I dare say he did. And there's your chance, if you've got the guts to take it. He's told Hatty he might as well put a bullet through his brain, he's on your neck for keeps—he wasn't really a very nice young man, I'm afraid, I don't blame Hatty for saying she wouldn't marry him for all the tea in China—he's worse than a ball and chain because you can hope to shuffle that off some time. So—how about a glass of beer ? And into the kitchen, and while he's getting you some lemonade or something you dunk the tablets in the drink and—what then ? You slip the empty phial in your pocket, and you forget about it. And when you remember it, when the police start asking awkward questions, it's too late to find it accidentally, so it can't be suicide, but your luck holds, when the balloon goes up Hatty Savage is the passenger, and you can breathe again. Only then Marguerite Grey moves in. Crime's so disheartening I often wonder why chaps go on sticking to it."

" You can't prove any of that," said Alison. " And if you're any kind of a lawyer you know it."

" There's still Marguerite. She made you a present of the situation, didn't she ? Of course she told you she was going to dress up, she wanted your help in getting into her glad rags, then you say—or she says—' I'll sit here, these dollies are my refugee children '—and you say, ' How about a shawl ? All refugees need a shawl and I've got the very thing.' Anyone notice that the shawl was over the knife, it hadn't been pierced, the shawl was only put on after death ? "

" Why put it on at all ? " asked Henrietta.

" Well, a shawl's a very useful thing for concealing a weapon, and if she'd seen Miss Sheridan pick up a carving knife she might have started wondering what it was all about."

" Why didn't she see her ? " inquired Lady Martin. " There's a glass on the wall. When the knife was taken from the table . . ."

" Who said anything about the table ? " He looked down

at plates and cutlery they had set there. " I don't see any knife now and this is supposed to be a copy of the way it was that day."

" Well, of course not," discovered Henrietta. " You don't have knives at a fork luncheon. That's the idea of it. You have a plate in one hand and a fork in the other . . ."

" So whoever was responsible for stabbing Miss Grey had to fetch the knife from the kitchen and no one except Mrs. Savage had ever been there or probably knew where it was. But you'd need an excuse to get the knife and what better than the shawl. I wonder if Marguerite knew what was happening to her ? " he went on, drawing his thick brows together. " Unless she happened to look in the glass she wouldn't know what hit her. Cobb, I think Mrs. Savage could do with a drop of brandy or something."

" You'll find it in the sideboard," said Alison. " May we take it that you have a tape-recorder concealed in the room ? "

" I've got six witnesses," Crook reminded her. " I've got the picture, I've got Louie Marsh, that's her married name, to swear that it represents Dickie Smith, I've got the fact that a couple of local calls were put through from your private office at The Clover House at midday on the day in question, and if need be I'll find a witness who saw Mrs. Cobb mending that car at twelve-thirty, if I have to make him myself out of a dog's inside and a lump of coal."

Philip Cobb, who had been helping Henrietta to pour out the drinks, now began to pass them round.

" If Marguerite was expecting my client to bring a sizable wad of notes with her I dare say she'd have the letters handy," Crook reflected, giving a glass to the doomed woman. " Wouldn't take long to dump them in the fire, making sure they could be identified, and then beetle off and catch the bus."

" Really, Mr. Crook, anyone might think you were there yourself." Alison lifted her glass. Crook was watching her lynx-eyed, but the handkerchief was back in her pocket and her hands seemed empty. " Poor Marguerite, she was sur- prised." With a gesture like light she flung the contents of her glass into Crook's face. For a moment he was the focus of everyone's attention.

"Watch her," yelled Crook, but he was too late. Moving like a deer she was across the room, had flung up the window and had dived out. There was a stone rockery below, and though she was still living when they picked her up she didn't recover to make a statement.

"Did you really think Philip might be guilty?" Henrietta asked him, after the police had done their stuff, and gone off with baleful glances at the man who'd let a criminal escape their clutches.

"I'm like Sir Thomas Howard," confessed Crook. "'Fore God, I am no coward. But even so I'd jib at accusin' a man in love of tryin' to destroy his wife. No, I just told him to play along with me, no matter what road I took. No sense buying a dog and barking yourself," he added, "and I was being hired to represent his interests."

"And the hundred pounds?" Henrietta suggested. "Did you ever find out where Richard got that?"

"From his auntie, of course. I wouldn't have minded being there disguised as a curtain-hook or something when he came back from Leffingham that day. Whether he told her right away about Marguerite or not, I don't know. He could just have said he'd got into conversation with someone and she, knowing she was guilty as hell, would have to play ball."

"But she went round everywhere asking about the money," Henrietta protested.

"Ever seen a lady lapwing try to lure you from her nest? Never saw such a commotion, whereas the truth is if she'd imitated Brer Rabbit, laid low and said nuffin, the odds are you wouldn't even have noticed her. Mind you, it was a nasty situation for her. Obtaining money under false pretences. She had no right to a penny of her brother's money once she knew the boy was dead. He could have put the heat on for ever and ever."

"What good would that have done him?"

"He didn't have to bother about that. He knew she'd

pay. And she was worse off than a chap who's got a lifer because he can get remission for good behaviour, but she was never going to have a day's freedom so long as that little rat was alive. He could insist on being made a sleeping partner, he could demand a joint banking account, we don't know, and now we never will, the scope of his demands. If you want my candid opinion, most people that get themselves murdered ask for it; certainly these two did, and in my opinion Miss Sheridan was worth half a dozen of them —till she made it clear she was willing to let my client bear the brunt."

" That's what I don't understand," confessed Henrietta. " How she could let Hatty be blamed twice."

" Why, what was Hatty to her ? There's no one so single-minded as your murderer. Well, if he didn't think his affairs were more important than another fellow's life he wouldn't have struck the fatal blow in the first place."

It was Crook who went down to the prison to collect Hatty when she was released.

" I don't want anyone," Hatty had declared, frozen and ungrateful. " I'm sick of being a raree-show. First it was, ' Come and look at the girl who killed Marguerite Grey and probably poisoned Richard Sheridan.' Now it'll be, ' Come and look at the girl that clever Mr. Crook got off.' I'm innocent, innocent, do you hear, and I won't be stared at."

" Lawyers don't count as people," Crook soothed her. " And what hope do you imagine you've got of walking out alone ? Unless they let you pack your robe of invisibility, and that don't sound like the police. Why, you'd have the Press round you nearer than your skin and more dangerous than a pack of horse-flies. And, seeing you're going to pay my professional expenses, let me give you a last tip, free, gratis and for nothing. If your husband's set his heart on buying that practice up north, you back him up. Husbands are like caterpillars, they improve with keeping, and you could have picked a lot worse."

" It's obvious you've never been married for charity," fired Hatty.

"You don't read your Bible enough," he told her. "You couldn't be married for a better reason."

"It's always the old maids and bachelors who know most about that kind of thing," she jeered.

"Well, what d'you expect? They're the only ones who haven't had a chance of getting the gilt rubbed off their ginger-bread."

He drew the Old Superb up at the corner of Bridge Street. "You can drop me here," Hatty had told him ungraciously. "I'll walk the last few steps."

She got out practically without a word of acknowledgment. He saw she was shaking like the proverbial aspen.

"Labourer's worthy of his hire," he thought philosophically, "but he don't rate a kind word by way of a tip. Oh well, she don't approve of charity. She just said so."

Philip Cobb had seen the car approaching and was waiting a few steps away. Hatty stiffened. She had wondered what his first words would be. Thank God! She couldn't stand an emotional scene and he might as well know it. That great Cheshire Cat, Crook, as pleased as Punch. . . .

His first words gave her a shock. "I hope you were civil to Crook," he said.

"Crook?" She stared. "He's being paid, isn't he?"

"You can't value your life much if you don't rate it higher than a lawyer's bill."

"Well," muttered Hatty, defiantly, "why should I?"

"Come inside," he invited her, "and I'll tell you."

"Wait a minute. There's something I have to say first. If you want your freedom, it can be fixed, I'm sure it can. I should understand perfectly and I shall be all right, only I don't want a lot of sickening pity. . . ."

"You don't understand a thing," her husband told her. "You seem to think a couple of ridiculous infatuations are the beginning and the end of existence. Just two men out of the whole world, and you're prepared to lie down and give them best. Why, you haven't begun to understand anything about love yet."

She didn't crumple. Crook would have liked that.

"I suppose you think you can teach me."

" No one else is going to get the chance. Mind you, you're dumb. You don't even know love when you meet it face to face."

" I don't want to hear any more about it," she flamed.

" Then you'd better buy yourself a pair of ear-muffs, because you're going to hear precious little else during the months to come. We're going north in about a fortnight— I've only been waiting for your signature . . ."

" You were sure you'd get it ? "

" Of course. You had Crook behind you, you couldn't lose."

" Oh, don't be so sickeningly modest," she told him. " It's not Crook I'm interested in. It's you. He was being employed to back me, but you—you actually believed me."

" For a girl who doesn't like publicity you're coming along very nicely," her husband teased, and now at last she did agree to come into the house.

Crook, watching from the corner and aware that behind every curtain in the road lurked a creature about as harmless as a leopard, slammed the door of the car and stood on the accelerator.

" I shall have to add Matrimonial Agent to my card," he said aloud, as the big yellow Rolls bounded forward like Boadicea's chariot advancing to destroy her country's enemies.